MR HARTINGTON DIED TOMORROW

Francis Durbridge

writing as

Lewis Middleton Harvey

WILLIAMS & WHITING

Applications for performance or other rights should be made
to The Agency, 24 Pottery Lane, London W11 4LZ.

Cover design by Timo Schroeder

9781912582570

Williams & Whiting (Publishers)
15 Chestnut Grove, Hurstpierpoint,
West Sussex, BN6 9SS

Titles by Francis Durbridge published by Williams & Whiting

1   The Scarf – tv serial
2   Paul Temple and the Curzon Case – radio serial
3   La Boutique – radio serial
4   The Broken Horseshoe – tv serial
5   Three Plays for Radio Volume 1
6   Send for Paul Temple – radio serial
7   A Time of Day – tv serial
8   Death Comes to The Hibiscus – stage play
    The Essential Heart – radio play
    (writing as Nicholas Vane)
9   Send for Paul Temple – stage play
10 The Teckman Biography – tv serial
11 Paul Temple and Steve – radio serial
12 Twenty Minutes From Rome – a teleplay
13 Portrait of Alison – tv serial
14 Paul Temple: Two Plays for Radio Volume 1
15 Three Plays for Radio Volume 2
16 The Other Man – tv serial
17 Paul Temple and the Spencer Affair – radio serial
18 Step In The Dark – film script
19 My Friend Charles – tv serial
20 A Case For Paul Temple – radio serial
21 Murder In The Media – more rediscovered serials and
    stories
22 The Desperate People – tv serial
23 Paul Temple: Two Plays for Television
24 And Anthony Sherwood Laughed – radio series
25 The World of Tim Frazer – tv serial
26 Paul Temple Intervenes – radio serial
27 Passport To Danger! – radio serial
28 Bat Out of Hell – tv serial
29 Send For Paul Temple Again – radio serial

Murder At The Weekend – the rediscovered newspaper serials and short stories

Also published by Williams & Whiting:
Francis Durbridge : The Complete Guide
By Melvyn Barnes

Titles by Francis Durbridge to be published by Williams & Whiting

A Game of Murder
A Man Called Harry Brent
Breakaway – The Family Affair
Breakaway – The Local Affair
Farewell Leicester Square (writing as Lewis Middleton Harvey)
Five Minute Mysteries (includes Michael Starr Investigates and The Memoirs of Andre d'Arnell)
Johnny Washington Esquire
Melissa
Murder On The Continent (Further re-discovered serials and stories)
One Man To Another – a novel
Operation Diplomat
Paul Temple and the Alex Affair
Paul Temple and the Canterbury Case (film script)
Paul Temple and the Conrad Case
Paul Temple and the Geneva Mystery
Paul Temple and the Gilbert Case
Paul Temple and the Gregory Affair
Paul Temple and the Jonathan Mystery
Paul Temple and the Lawrence Affair
Paul Temple and the Madison Mystery
Paul Temple and the Margo Mystery
Paul Temple and the Sullivan Mystery
Paul Temple and the Vandyke Affair
Paul Temple: Two Plays For Radio Vol 2 (Send For Paul Temple and News of Paul Temple)
The Doll
The Female of the Species (The Girl at the Hibiscus and Introducing Gail Carlton)

The Man From Washington
The Passenger
Tim Frazer and the Salinger Affair
Tim Frazer and the Mellin Forrest Mystery

INTRODUCTION

Many will remember Francis Durbridge (1912-98) as a prolific writer of mystery serials for BBC radio and television, and particularly for his creation of the novelist/detective Paul Temple and his wife Steve in their pursuits of murderous criminals with menacing sobriquets. But far fewer will know that for his radio work Durbridge occasionally used the pseudonyms Frank Cromwell, Nicholas Vane and Lewis Middleton Harvey.

Before looking at his pseudonymous radio contributions, perhaps a brief résumé of Durbridge's career will be helpful in putting him in context - given that his first radio credit on 25 July 1933, *The Three-Cornered Hat*, was a play for children that was far removed from the crime genre which later gave him international renown. Although most of his early radio works were aimed at children or were light entertainments, including libretti for musical comedies, his first serious drama *Promotion* was broadcast on 3 October 1934 and a talent for crime fiction became evident in his plays *Murder in the Midlands* (1934) and *Murder in the Embassy* (1937). Then in 1938 his serial *Send for Paul Temple* proved so successful that many sequels were broadcast until 1968, establishing an enormous UK and European fanbase.

Many of his serials were novelised, but Durbridge regarded himself primarily as a playwright and pursued his craft by contributing to BBC radio for very many years. Then in 1952, while continuing to write for radio, he embarked on a sequence of BBC television serials (not featuring the Temples) that achieved huge viewing figures until 1980. But even more, from 1971 in the UK and beginning even earlier in Germany, he wrote nine intriguing stage plays.

His use of pseudonyms might take longstanding fans by surprise. The earliest example was "Frank Cromwell", with a double bill of plays called *Crash* and *Gay Interlude* (broadcast on 12 June 1935, produced by Martyn C. Webster) that credited *Crash* to Frank Cromwell although *Gay Interlude* was credited to Durbridge! In fact *Crash* had a longer life, with a new production again credited to Frank Cromwell included in a triple bill of plays broadcast on 19 September 1935 (again produced by Webster). But it later reappeared in a new guise as the twenty-five minute play *Information Received* (broadcast on 25 February 1938), produced by Howard Rose, which included the same characters as the 1935 *Crash* but this time credited Durbridge as the writer. And in the meantime, the pseudonymous Frank Cromwell had been involved in a one-hour musical comedy *Sauce for the Gander* (broadcast on 14 July 1936, produced by Martyn C. Webster), with the libretto credited to Durbridge and the song lyrics to Cromwell!

As "Nicholas Vane" Durbridge wrote (jointly with Val Gielgud) six fifteen-minute radio mysteries called *The Girl at the Hibiscus* (broadcast 22 August to 26 September 1941), with Gielgud producing the first episode and Martyn C. Webster the others. This was quickly followed by a radio serial of twelve fifteen-minute episodes (again credited to Nicholas Vane and Val Gielgud, broadcast from 28 November 1941 to 20 February 1942) called *Death Comes to the Hibiscus*, produced by Webster. Then his third radio contribution as Nicholas Vane was a twenty-minute romantic comedy about a failing marriage, *The Essential Heart*, produced by Val Gielgud and broadcast on 6 February 1943 – and some years later, on 22 March 1952, a new production of *The Essential Heart* was broadcast, this time produced by Trafford Whitelock and still credited to Nicholas Vane. And Durbridge's final use of the Vane pseudonym was another series of short plays, *Introducing Gail Carlton*, broadcast from 10 December 1943 to 21 January 1944 in six fifteen-minute episodes. These adventures of a newspaper reporter during the then-current war were produced by the ever-present Webster.

So what of Durbridge's pseudonym "Lewis Middleton Harvey"? This was only used for two radio serials - *Mr Hartington Died Tomorrow* (9 February – 6 April 1942, eight thirty-minute episodes, produced by Val Gielgud) and *Farewell, Leicester Square!* (8 February – 29 March 1943, eight twenty-minute episodes, produced by Martyn C. Webster). The latter, incidentally, was not a thriller serial but the story of a theatrical company that might possibly have been inspired (and I speculate) by the longstanding success of J.B. Priestley's 1929 novel *The Good Companions*.

It is intriguing that *Mr Hartington Died Tomorrow* was previewed in the *Radio Times* (15 August 1941) with the description "a serial play by a new author, dealing with life (and murder!) in Hollywood's English colony." Very evidently, therefore, the true identity of Lewis Middleton Harvey was being concealed at that time. Nevertheless, when *Farewell, Leicester Square!* was previewed (*Radio Times*, 29 January 1943) it was described as "a new serial play of eight instalments, by Francis Durbridge of Paul Temple fame." While factually correct, this revelation was a slip that the BBC was quick to rectify - and Lewis Middleton Harvey was credited in subsequent issues of the *Radio Times* for each serial episode with no mention whatsoever of Durbridge.

A new production of *Mr Hartington Died Tomorrow*, abridged to just one hour, was broadcast on 30 October 1942 and was again credited to Harvey and produced by Gielgud. But this plot had a long life, as a further production of the full eight episodes was broadcast from 31 January to 21 March 1950, again credited to Harvey but produced by David H. Godfrey (although Webster was script editor). A point of interest arising from this 1950 production is that Peter Coke played the mysterious Peter London with Marjorie Westbury in a small role, and four years later they were to get together for the first time as Paul and Steve Temple in *Paul Temple and the Gilbert Case*. The rest is history, as they say.

So Francis Durbridge fans, and indeed the wider crime fiction community, now have the opportunity after eighty years to learn how *Mr Hartington Died Tomorrow*.

Melvyn Barnes
Author of *Francis Durbridge: The Complete Guide* (Williams & Whiting, 2018)

This book reproduces Francis Durbridge's original script together with the list of characters and actors of the BBC programme on the dates mentioned, but the eventual broadcast might have edited Durbridge's script in respect of scenes, dialogue and character names.

MR HARTINGTON DIED TOMORROW

A serial in eight episodes

By FRANCIS DURBRIDGE

Writing as

LEWIS MIDDLETON HARVEY

Broadcast on BBC Radio

9 February – 6 April 1942

CAST:

Dallas Shale . . . . .James McKechnie
Campbell Mansfield . . . Laidman Browne
Charlie . . . . G R Schjelderup
Julius Markham . . . . . . .Alexander Sarner
Margaret Freeman . . . . . Grizelda Hervey
Doris Charleston . . . . . . Tucker McGuire
Louis Cheyne . . . . Malcolm Graeme
Mary Brampton . . . . Olga Edwards
Gail Howard . . . . Phyllis Calvert
Sam Levinsky . . . . Ernest Sefton
Div Inspector O'Hara . . Harry Hutchinson
Peter London . . . . Philip Cunningham
Sergeant Moore . . . . Roy Emerton
A girl . . . . .Joan Miller
First car driver (' Ed ') . . . . . .Jack Livesey
Second car driver . . . . .Ernest Sefton
Sergeant Quinn . . . . Allan Jeayes
A Janitor . . . . Ernest Sefton
Alderman Love . . . . .Allan Jeayes

Tom Love . . . . Jack Livesey
Maisie .Joan Miller
Joe Francino . . . . Dino Galvani
Jock Reid . . . . .John Laurie
Waitress . . . . .Muriel Pratt
Mr Regan . . . . .Jack Livesey
First girl . . . . Lucille Lisle
Second girl . . . . .Joan Miller
Third girl . . . . Viki Dobson
Leo Bartlett . . . . .Heron Carvic
Sam . . . . .Macdonald Parke
A man . . . . Ernest Sefton
Spencer . . . . Ernest Sefton
Sylvestor . . . . Andrea Melandrinos
Dr Latimer . . . . Ivan Samson
Sergeant Dane . . . . .Jack Livesey
Radio Announcer . . . . Joan Miller
Henry K Hammerston . . . . Roy Emerton
Horace Wyndham Harringford . John Laurie
A man . . . . .G R Schjelderup
Jane Wise . . . . Connie Burnett
Radio announcer . . . . .Allan Jeayes
Larry . . . . Allan Jeayes
Otto Stultz . . . . Ernest Sefton
Joe . . . . Jack Livesey
Tony .Bryan Herbert
Dr Team . . . . .Finlay Currie
First American . . . . .Roy Emerton
Second Voice . . . . Jack Livesey
Third Voice . . . . Joan Miller
Fourth Voice . . . . Allan Jeayes

NEW PRODUCTION
abridged to one hour
30 October 1942
CAST:

Dallas Shale . . . . James McKechnie
Campbell Mansfield . . . . . . .Laidman Browne
Charlie . . . . .Preston Lockwood
Julius Markham . . . . .Alexander Sarner
Doris Charleston . . . . Naomi Campbell
Margaret Freeman . . . . .Grizelda Hervey
Louis Cheyne . . . . Malcolm Graeme
Gail Howard . . . . .Penelope Davidson
Div Inspector O'Hara . . . . . Harry Hutchinson
A doctor . . . . .Richard Williams
Sgt Moore . . . . .Tony Quinn
Peter London . . . . .Philip Cunningham
Leo Bartlett . . . . .Max Adrian
First radio announcer . . . . Rita Vale
Second radio announcer . . . . .Harry Ross
Otto Stultz . . . . Ernest Sefton
Dr Team . . . . .Richard Williams

NEW PRODUCTION
31 January – 21 March 1950
CAST:

Dallas Shale . . . . .Douglass Montgomery
Campbell Mansfield . . . . . . .Richard Williams
Julius Markham . . . . .Leo de Pokorny
Margaret Freeman . . . . Grizelda Hervey
Doris Charleston . . . . Rita Vale
Louis Cheyne . . . . Hamilton Dyce
Gail Howard . . . . Catherine Campbell
Div Inspector O'Hara . . . . Tommy Duggan
Peter London . . . . .Peter Coke
Charlie . . . . .Jon Farrell
Sam Livinsky . . . . .Ian Sadler
Doctor . . . . Bryan Powley
Sergeant Moore . . . . .John McClaren
Waiter . . . . .Charles Leno
Mary Brampton . . . . Elizabeth Maude
Sergeant Quinn . . . . .Charles Leno
Maisie . . . . .Janet Morrison
Joe Francino . . . . Roger Snowdon
Jock Reid . . . . .Duncan McIntyre
Tom Love . . . . Richard Hurndall
Alderman Love . . . . Bryan Powley
Leo Bartlett . . . . Ivan Samson
Mr Regan . . . . Macdonald Parke
Spencer . . . . Eddy Reed
Sylvester . . . . Alastair Duncan
Lionel . . . . .Richard Hurndall
Sergeant Dane . . . . .John Drexler
Henry K Hammerston . . . . Frank Coburn
Dr Latimer . . . . .John Richmond
First radio announcer . . . . Warren Stanhope

EPISODE ONE

MR HARTINGTON'S SIESTA

MAN: Two thousand, seven hundred and fifty-four
                    miles from New York City in the State of
                    California there is a place called ...
                    Hollywood.

FADE UP music to a dramatic crescendo.

*As the music finishes the first notes of a cuckoo clock can be
heard.*

                    Cuckoo! Cuckoo! Cuckoo! Cuckoo!
                    Cuckoo! Cuckoo! Cuckoo! Cuckoo!
Fade the clock.

FADE UP music to a dramatic crescendo.

1st AMERICAN: (*Pleasantly: surprised tone*) Hello, there!!!!
                 This is Jackie Wendlemen, the Voice of
                 Hollywood! Welcome to Los Angeles,
                 folks!!!
2nd VOICE: (*Booming: declamatory*) STATISTICS!!!!
1st AMERICAN: One hundred and fifty-seven film studios!
2nd VOICE: Sixteen hundred divorces!!!!
1st AMERICAN: Three hundred and seventy-eight swimming
                 pools!!!!
2nd VOICE: Nine thousand, two hundred and twenty-four
                 vegetarians!!!!
1st AMERICAN: Sixteen thousand, three hundred and ninety-
                 seven automobiles!!
2nd VOICE: (*Booming: declamatory*) STATISTICS!!!!
3rd VOICE: (*Softly*) Phooey!
*A quick flash of music ... Slaughter On Tenth Avenue by Rodgers
and Hart*

4th VOICE:	(*With a strange charm*) Quote: "I had been warned many times by American friends that I must expect to find a mushroom-town filled to overflowing with exquisitely beautiful young ladies. My first impression was that Los Angeles is a toadstool-town filled to overflowing with centenarians." Unquote.

Quick flash of music.
FADE DOWN.

5th VOICE:	(*Common American: quickly*) Variety!!!! Flash! "Clark Gable at Para on four-pix deal!" Flash! "H.G.T. shelves Wagner." Flash! "Rooney says 'No dice' to M.O.K. unit." Flash! "Bob Taylor laffs …"

FADE.

Quick flash of music … FADE DOWN.

4th VOICE:	(*Friendly: jovial*) Don't forget to eat at Joe's Place … Mary had a little lamb: what will you have?

Quick flash of music …. FADE DOWN.

6th MAN:	(*Shouting*) Scene Six … Take four …

A clapper board is heard.

4th VOICE:	O.K. for Sound!!!!
6th MAN:	Camera!!!!
GIRL:	(*Sweetly*) Three words, dear Romeo, and goodnight indeed. If that thy bent of love be honourable, Thy purpose marriage, send me word tomorrow, By one that I'll procure to …
6th MAN:	(*Shouting*) Cut!!! Cut!!!
GIRL:	(*Tough*) Now what's wrong …?
6th MAN:	It stinks!

Quick flash of music.
FADE DOWN.

A WOMAN:	(*Very disappointed*) So this … is Hollywood.

4

Musical flash.

FADE to background.

4th VOICE: Semi-tropical flowers, rich in fragrance and colour ...

5th VOICE: White stucco houses and hospitable, unfenced lawns ...

4th VOICE: Arid desert and snow-capped mountains ...

FADE UP of music.

5th VOICE: Cruel cactus, and friendly orange groves ...

4th VOICE: The Trocadero ... Sunset Boulevard.

5th VOICE: La Brea Avenue ... The Clover Club ... Harpo's Bar ... The Hollywood Punch Bowl.

4th VOICE: Wilshire Boulevard ... The Blue Stetson ... Charlie's Snuggery ...

5th VOICE: Joe's Place ...

4th VOICE: The Garden of Allah ...

FADE IN of music.

A WOMAN: (*Disappointed: almost contemptuously*) So this ... is Hollywood!

The music reaches a dramatic crescendo and then the cuckoo clock is heard.

Cuckoo! Cuckoo! Cuckoo! Cuckoo! Cuckoo!

When the clock finishes DALLAS SHALE speaks.

SHALE: I'll have another highball, Charlie.

CHARLIE: It's your stomach, brother. (*He mixes the drink*) Aren't you going to the preview?

SHALE: What preview?

CHARLIE: Over at the Matamount. It's a sneak show. Strictly a surprise all round. There's Isn't a guy in Tibet that knows a thing about it.

SHALE: Don't let's talk about pictures, Charlie. Remember we are men of breeding, men of culture ...

5

CHARLIE:	You said it! (*Passing the drink*) One highball …
SHALE:	Skoal! (*He drinks and gives a sigh of satisfaction*) Ah!
CHARLIE:	If you take my tip you'll lay off …
SHALE:	(*Confidentially*) Once, many years ago, Charlie, I wrote a book …
CHARLIE:	You've kinda mentioned it before, Mr Shale.
SHALE:	A real book … A real book, Charlie. The Forgotten Street by Dallas Shale … Think of it, Charlie … Fifteen chapters … Ninety-five thousand words … Ninety-five thousand words …
CHARLIE:	(*Bored*) You think of it, brother – it's your book.
SHALE:	(*Rather sentimental*) The Forgotten Street by Dallas Shale … (*Pulling himself together*) Yeah – the same again, Charlie.
CHARLIE:	Now just a minute, Mr Shale, you've had seven highballs, and … (*Suddenly*) Hello, look who's here …
SHALE:	You mean the little guy in the grey suit?
CHARLIE:	Yeah … Campbell Mansfield … the man who wrote The Canterbury Saga?
SHALE:	Campbell Mansfield …? What's he doing in Hollywood?
CHARLIE:	They say he's under contract to Julius Markham.
SHALE:	Chee! I guess that's progress.

There is a tiny pause.

MANSFIELD:	Good evening.
CHARLIE:	Good evening, sir.
MANSFIELD:	Can I have a brandy and ginger ale?

CHARLIE:	Certainly, sir. (*Mixing drink*) Kind of warm …
MANSFIELD:	Yes. Yes, it is rather …
SHALE:	How do you like our climate, Mr Mansfield?
MANSFIELD:	(*Pleasantly*) It's a case of having to like it.
SHALE:	My name's Shale. Dallas Shale … Feature writer for the Ross-Morgan Syndicate in San Francisco.
MANSFIELD:	Oh – er – how do you do?
CHARLIE:	One highball.
SHALE:	Oh, thanks, Charlie. When did you arrive, Mr Mansfield?
MANSFIELD:	Ten thirty this morning. And you …?
SHALE:	I arrived in Hollywood on September 4th, 1931, at precisely six thirty-five in the evening. It was raining like Hell.
MANSFIELD:	(*Slightly amused*) You don't care for Hollywood, Mr Shale?
SHALE:	Oh, yes. Yes, I'm crazy about Hollywood. It's just like home … just like home. (*As an afterthought*) There's no place like it.
MANSFIELD:	I suppose you handle most of the publicity stories, interviews with the stars, and that sort of thing?
SHALE:	That's the ticket! What Miss X had for breakfast and who she had it with.
MANSFIELD:	(*Puzzled*) But is that why you came out to Hollywood in the first place – I mean, to do that sort of thing?
SHALE:	Not exactly. I came out here on the same game as yourself. Contract writer for H.G.T. Twelve hundred dollars a week. Wet or fine. Work or play.

MANSFIELD:	I'm actually under contract to Julius Markham. I don't know whether you know Markham or not?
SHALE:	Yeah! Yeah, I know Markham. He's a swell talker. The guy with the silver tongue.
MANSFIELD:	I like Julius Markham. Oh, I know he's a quixotic sort of person, but he gets ideas. The right kind of ideas. Actually it was Julius Markham who finally persuaded me to come out to Hollywood.
SHALE:	(*Quietly*) Did you read his article last week in Variety?
MANSFIELD:	Yes, and he's right, Shale! Make no mistake about it, he's right!
SHALE:	How come?
MANSFIELD:	The trouble with pictures at the moment is the material or − shall we say − the lack of material. Whichever way you look at it, Shale, Hollywood has <u>got</u> to have new stories.
SHALE:	I guess this is where I came in!
MANSFIELD:	What do you mean?
SHALE:	Mr Mansfield, since the days of Pearl White and Buster Keaton, Hollywood and men like Julius Markham have been demanding new stories and new ideas. Hundreds and thousands of writers have come to Hollywood from London, Paris, Berlin, Prague, New York, Chicago, Detroit, Michigan, Kansas, and all points west; and still, my dear Mr Mansfield … Boy meets Girl. And make no mistake about it, the same boy meets the same girl.
MANSFIELD:	(*Puzzled*) Does that mean that you don't − er − believe in bringing new writers to

8

	Hollywood? In literally combing the Continent for new stories and new …
SHALE:	It isn't a case of what guys like me believe in, Mr Mansfield. It's simply a case of what the big noises say! Julius Markham wants new stories … O.K! Julius Markham insists on new stories … O.K! But does Mr Julius Gabriel Sydney Markham realise that <u>here</u> … <u>here</u> in Hollywood … right under his illustrious nose, is the greatest story of all time? The story of Oliver Hartington. The Man who died … tomorrow?

Slight pause.

MANSFIELD:	Oliver Hartington? I remember that story. Hartington was found dead in a Hollywood restaurant at one o'clock in the morning. The news was telephoned all over the world and the newspapers brought out a special edition.
SHALE:	That's right. Although Hartington was found dead in The Blue Stetson restaurant on Tuesday morning it was still Monday evening there, so the newspapers carried the headline: "Mr Hartington Died Tomorrow".
MANSFIELD:	Yes, but surely the Hartington business was pretty straight forward? The newspapers …
SHALE:	The newspapers went completely haywire. They described Hartington as the greatest film genius of all time. The Czar of Hollywood!
MANSFIELD:	And wasn't he?
SHALE:	(*After a tiny pause: with a laugh*) I'm darned if I know!
MANSFIELD:	But you knew Mr Hartington?

SHALE:	Oh, yeah. Yeah, I knew Hartington all right. As a matter of fact my office was only about five yards away from Carnegie Hall.
MANSFIELD:	(*Surprised*) Carnegie Hall?
SHALE:	(*Suddenly laughing*) Oh … that's what we used to call Hartington's private snuggery. (*Amused*) Boy, you've never seen an office like it.
MANSFIELD:	I know that Hartington was President of the H.G.T. Corporation, and Vice-President of the M.O.M. and Broadway-Sun syndicates … (*Puzzled*) But what exactly did he do?
SHALE:	(*Aghast*) What exactly did he do? (*Amazed*) Oliver Hartington?
MANSFIELD:	Yes.
SHALE:	(*Bewildered*) Well, I … I don't exactly know what he … er actually did. I mean, Hartington was the big noise in Hollywood … the real big noise … no one kind of got around to asking him what he actually did.
MANSFIELD:	Yes, but … wasn't it pretty obvious?
SHALE:	Obvious? Good God, no!
MANSFIELD:	But he must have done something!
SHALE:	Well, I reckon he collected close on four hundred thousand dollars a year; and it was always pretty difficult to see him, even by appointment.
MANSFIELD:	Then, at least, he always appeared to be busy?
SHALE:	Appeared to be busy? He had forty-seven buttons on his desk, Mr Mansfield … in other words forty-seven buzzers … and boy, when Hartington was in the mood, how he could buzz!

A pause.

10

MANSFIELD:	Did you like Mr Hartington?
SHALE:	Like him? Well, I sent the guy twenty dollars' worth of orchids when he passed out!

CAMPBELL MANSFIELD laughs.

MANSFIELD:	(*To CHARLIE*) The same again … A little while ago you said …
SHALE:	(*Quietly*) … I said … the story of Oliver Hartington is the greatest story of all time. (*A tiny pause*) Yeah … Yeah … I know … I guess I was talking out of turn.

A pause.

MANSFIELD:	Mr Shale …
SHALE:	Yeah?
MANSFIELD:	What is the true story of … Oliver Hartington?

A slight pause.

SHALE:	In the spring on 1938, Hartington announced that he had decided to make a film based on an unknown novel, written by a man named Peter London, and called The Modern Pilgrim. Unfortunately, however, no one knew anything at all about Peter London, and every attempt by the studio executives to locate the guy met with failure. Hartington was wild with anger. Talent Scouts and H.G.T. officials from Bangkok to Baghdad offered fantastic sums for information which might lead them to the hideout of the illusive author …

A quick flash of music … then FADE it to the background.

The sound of numerous, frantic, desk buzzers, telephones, typewriters, etc are heard.
The GIRLS speak in a mechanical sing-song …

1st GIRL:	Sorry, Mr Hartington, no news of Peter London!
2nd GIRL:	Sorry, Mr Hartington, no news of Peter London!
3rd GIRL:	Hollywood calling Chicago … Hollywood calling Chicago …
4th GIRL:	Go ahead Stockholm … Go ahead Stockholm … Hollywood calling Stockholm … Hollywood calling Stockholm …
1st MAN:	(*Urgently*) Any news of Peter London? Any news of Peter London? Any news of Peter London? Any news of Peter London? Any news of … (*FADE voice*)
3rd GIRL:	Hold the line New York … Hold the line, New York … Go ahead New York … Go ahead New York.
4th GIRL:	Hollywood calling London … Hollywood calling London …
3rd GIRL:	Hold the line, Geneva … Hold the line, Geneva … Hollywood calling Geneva … Hollywood calling Geneva …
1st MAN:	(*Urgently*) Any news of Peter London? Any news of Peter London? Any news of Peter London? Any news of … (*FADE voice*)
4th GIRL:	Hold the line, Cape Town … Hollywood calling Cape Town … Hold the line, Cape Town … Hollywood calling Cape town …
1st GIRL:	Sorry, Mr Hartington, no news of Peter London!
2nd GIRL:	Sorry, Mr Hartington, no news of Peter London!
1st GIRL:	Sorry, Mr Hartington, no news of Peter London!

2nd GIRL: Sorry, Mr Hartington, no news of Peter London!

1st GIRL: Sorry, Mr Hartington, no news of ... (*FADE voice*)

A quick flash of music ...

FADE DOWN for the voice of DALLAS SHALE.

SHALE: But nothing happened, except that with each successive failure to find Peter London, Hartington grew angrier than ever. Then one night ... the night before the great man died ... I attended a script conference which was held in a board room adjoining Carnegie Hall. Hartington was not present but throughout the conference we could hear him summoning executives from the different floors. Doris Charleston, Hartington's confidential secretary, was present at the conference together with Julius Markham who was to direct the film ... the famous actress Margaret Freeman – who was tentatively scheduled to play the lead – and a colleague of mine, called Louis Cheyne, who ... (*FADE voice*)

FADE In of voices at the script conference.

The voices of JULIUS MARKHAM, MARGARET FREEMAN, DORIS CHARLESTON, LOUIS CHEYNE, and of course, DALLAS SHALE.

From the babble of voices LOUIS CHEYNE's is the first voice to be clearly heard. LOUIS is an Englishman.

LOUIS: (*Irritated*) I've never heard such stupid nonsense in all my life!

MARKHAM: (*He is a Russian Jew, and somewhat curt in manner*) Stupid or not, that's the position!

13

MARGARET: Oh, for heaven's sake, Louis! You know perfectly well that we can't do anything until we find Peter London, so ...

MARKHAM: Peter London! Peter London! I'm fed up with the sound of the guy's name! Why the Hell doesn't he show himself?

DORIS: I know one thing, Julius. This delay is certainly costing H.G.T. a pretty packet.

LOUIS: Hartington's just being obstinate!

DORIS: Well, the big man is certainly giving this production a great deal of thought. Larry Shuker tells me he sat for nearly two hours after lunch ... pondering over The Modern Pilgrim.

LOUIS: He always sits for two hours after a meal – especially if it happens to be in The Blue Stetson.

MARKHAM: Yeah, you know what the waiters call it; "Mr Hartington's Siesta!" ... the poor devils daren't disturb him for love nor money.

Suddenly, in the background, a buzzer is heard. There is a sudden silence.

MARGARET: (*Softly*) That's Hartington.

LOUIS: Who's he calling?

DORIS: Wait a minute!

The buzzer is heard for the second time.

DORIS: That's for Shackleton.

LOUIS: (*Surprised*) Shackleton? What on earth does he want Shackleton for?

MARKHAM: Somebody's got to re-write that scene!

LOUIS: Now listen to me, Markham, just because the script isn't full of phoney wisecracks, you've got the idea ...

DORIS: (*Calmly*) It's not a bit of use arguing over the script. If I've told you once, I've told you a hundred times, Hartington can't give the go-

14

	ahead signal until Peter London has actually sold the rights!
MARKHAM:	(*Angrily*) Then why the Hell call a script conference? Hartington treats the whole lot of us like a crowd of third rate … (*He is interrupted by the sound of a second buzzer from Hartington's office*) That's … that's Hartington again …
DORIS:	Yes.
SHALE:	Who's he calling this time?

The buzzer is repeated.

There is a slight pause.

DORIS:	That's for Bette Davis … unless I'm mistaken.
MARGARET:	(*Displeased*) Bette Davis?
LOUIS:	What's he doing now, re-casting the film?

A third buzzer is heard from Hartington's office.

SHALE:	What's that?
DORIS:	(*Surprised*) That's for one of the directors … I think it's … Mervyn.
MARKHAM:	Mervyn! Yeah, well I'm not taking orders from that Boston penpusher!
LOUIS:	Judging from the activity, Mr Hartington must have had a most inspiring siesta!

There is a knock, and the door opens.

DORIS:	Yes, Mary?
MARY:	There's a reply to your cable to New York, and also to the ones Mr Hartington sent to Melbourne and London.
DORIS:	Oh, good! Thank you, Mary.

The door closes.

MARGARET:	Let's hope this is good news – for a change.
MARKHAM:	Yeah.

A tiny pause.

LOUIS:	Well?

DORIS:	This is from Marshall in New York. (*Reading*) "Never heard of Peter London. Stop. Never heard of The Modern Pilgrim. Stop. Wish to God I'd never heard of Hollywood. Stop."
MARKHAM:	T't …
SHALE:	Wise guy! What do the London people say?
DORIS:	They're slightly more informative. (*Reading*) "Believe Peter London worked at British Museum nineteen-thirty. Stop. Left for Paris same year. Stop. No knowledge of present whereabouts. Stop. Regards … Carraway."
MARGARET:	And Melbourne?
DORIS:	(*Quietly – reading*) "No knowledge of Peter London. Stop. Suggest you try Sydney. Stop. Field."
LOUIS:	(*Irritated*) Suggest you try Sydney! Good God …
DORIS:	I've already tried Sydney … and Stockholm … and Lisbon … and Cape Town.

Another buzzer can be heard from Hartington's office – at first it is not noticed.

MARGARET:	What about the people who published the novel?
SHALE:	Yeah … that's an idea.
DORIS:	Hopeless! They've never even met Peter London.
MARKHAM:	Never even met him?
DORIS:	No. The novel didn't sell very well, you know.

The buzzer continues.

LOUIS:	I'm not surprised. Of all the pretentious, long winded …
SHALE:	(*Suddenly*) Say, listen!

There is a pause.

SHALE:	That's Hartington again …
MARKHAM:	(*Quietly*) Yeah.

16

The buzzer continues.

A slight pause.

SHALE: Sounds kind of heated.

MARKHAM: Who's he buzzing for?

DORIS: (*Puzzled*) I don't recognise that one ... at all.

The buzzer continues.

SHALE: He's going Hell – for – leather ... anyway.

DORIS: (*Suddenly*) Good God!

SHALE: What is it?

MARGARET: What's the matter?

DORIS: That's for me! (*Excitedly*) Gangway!!!!

The door opens and closes.

DALLAS SHALE is amused.

MARGARET: I wonder if Hartington intends to call the whole thing off?

MARKHAM: (*Annoyed*) What d'you mean ... call the whole thing off?

LOUIS: He can't do that – not now! We've spent nearly half a million on sets, and we haven't even started shooting!

MARGARET: Hartington can't go ahead until he's found this Peter London person, and actually <u>bought</u> the film rights – he's told me that himself! Yes, and if you want my opinion, if he doesn't find Peter London things are going to look pretty black – so far as we are concerned.

LOUIS: What do you mean ... so far as we are concerned?

MARGARET: (*Quietly*) I think you know what I mean, Louis.

LOUIS: (*Angrily*) I'm damned if I do!

SHALE: Let's be honest, Louis! You need this film ... we all need it. The last story you scripted for M.O.M. was a flop ... a one hundred per cent flop. The last picture Markham directed was a

17

	success … an artistic success … and you know what that means.
MARKHAM:	Say listen, Shale, there's no need to get personal. I'm here because it seems to me The Modern Pilgrim is a pretty good story for a director to …

The door opens.

MARGARET:	It's Doris!

A tiny pause.

LOUIS:	Well?
MARGARET:	What did he want?
DORIS:	You can relax … Hartington's leaving. He's driving down to The Blue Stetson.
MARKHAM:	Did he say anything?
DORIS:	Not a great deal. He's in what I call his impressionable mood. He'll probably doze for an hour or so after supper – then wake with an entirely new slant on things.
MARKHAM:	Yeah, and God knows what it'll be!
MARGARET:	The best thing we can do is …
LOUIS:	(*Interrupting MARGARET, away from the others*) There he goes!
DORIS:	Don't stand too near the window, Louis; he'll see you.

A slight pause.

MARKHAM:	(*Thoughtfully*) He's putting on weight.
SHALE:	Mr Oliver Hartington leaving for supper and siesta at The Blue Stetson! (*He speaks with sarcasm*)
MARGARET:	You sound as if you don't like Hartington?
SHALE:	I'm crazy about him!
MARKHAM:	Damn it, there's no need for <u>you</u> to be funny, Shale. Hartington <u>is</u> giving you a decent break!
SHALE:	(*Amazed*) A decent break?

A buzzer is heard from Carnegie Hall.

MARKHAM: Yeah – a decent break!

SHALE: My dear Julius, I'm down to write a two minute scene at the beginning of a third rate piece of pretentious tripe. However, if your somewhat limited intelligence chooses to consider that a ...

DORIS: (*Interrupting SHALE*) Be quiet!

The buzzer continues.

DORIS: Listen!

A pause.

The buzzer is heard once again.

MARKHAM: (*Amazed*) That's – that's from Hartington's office ...

MARGARET: But – but it can't be!

The buzzer continues.

LOUIS: (*Quickly*) The door's opening!

The door opens.

There is a tense pause.

GAIL HOWARD speaks. She is English, twenty-five and rather attractive.

GAIL: Good evening.

DORIS: (*Amazed*) Who – who are you? What do you want?

GAIL: I want to see Mr Hartington ... (*As an afterthought*) ... please.

DORIS: But – but how did you get up here?

GAIL: There was a door near the elevator ... it was open.

LOUIS: (*Quietly*) That's the private entrance, Hartington must have forgotten the door.

DORIS: Yes.

GAIL: I'm afraid I got rather panicky when I found myself in that office ... it's just a little overpowering, isn't it? (*She giggles*) I pressed a

lot of coloured buttons on the desk, I'm sorry if it
startled you.

DALLAS SHALE is amused.

DORIS: But – but who are you … exactly?

GAIL: My name is Howard … Gail Howard … I'm a
              writer.

LOUIS: But why do you want to see Mr Hartington?

GAIL: Well, I don't want to see Mr Hartington … not
              really. (*Faintly amused*) But I believe Mr
              Hartington wants to see me.

DORIS: To see you …?

GAIL: Yes. You see, I wrote one book under a
              pseudonym. It was called … The Modern
              Pilgrim.

MARKHAM: (*Astonished*) The … Modern … Pilgrim!

LOUIS: (*Staggered*) The … Modern … Pilgrim!

MARGARET: (*Bewildered*) You mean …?

DORIS: Then – then you're Peter London?

GAIL: (*Simply*) Yes, I'm Peter London.

*There is a sudden gasp of astonishment from DALLAS SHALE,
MARGARET, DORIS, MARKHAM and LOUIS. Before they
recover from their surprise however a wave of music surges in,
and as it fades away we hear the voice of DALLAS SHALE
telling the story to CAMPBELL MANSFIELD.*

SHALE: Talk about a surprise! Chee, I reckon you could
              have knocked the whole crowd of us down with
              a pocket dictionary!

MANSFIELD: (*Intrigued*) But … but what was she like this
              girl?

SHALE: Most attractive … and a swell sense of humour.
              Anyway, as soon as we realised exactly what had
              happened we all tumbled into Louis Cheyne's
              Packard and made straight for The Blue Stetson.

When we arrived at the restaurant, however, we got rather a shock, because the entire building was surrounded by …

FADE voice.
A wave of music surges in and FADES DOWN.

The car is heard drawing to a standstill. In the background can be heard loud excited voices … also the wail of police sirens …
The car ticks over …

MARKHAM: (*Surprised*) I say, what the Hell's going on around here?

DORIS: They've roped off the front entrance!

MARGARET: (*Puzzled*) Is it an accident …? I don't see anybody …

SHALE: Something's happened inside the place by the look of it!

MARKHAM: Yeah.

LOUIS: (*Calling*) Hi! Hi! Officer!!! (*He sounds his horn*)

DORIS: Who's this boy looking for?

MESSENGER: Are you people from H.G.T. Studios?

SHALE: Yeah.

MESSENGER: I've been chasing you for the last twenty minutes … Cable for Hartington … Sign please …

SHALE: O.K. (*Signing the form*) Say, what's all the fuss about?

MESSENGER: Search me! Thanks.

LOUIS: (*Sounding his horn again*) Hi!!! Hi, Sam!!!

SHALE: Lay off, Louis, or you'll land a ticket.

LOUIS: Not with this guy! (*Sounding his horn again*) Hi!!! Hi, Sam!!! (*Calling*) Sam!!! Sam Levinsky!!!

DORIS: He's spotted you!

A slight pause.
SAM LEVINSKY arrives.

21

SAM:	Hello, Mr Cheyne.
LOUIS:	Hello, Sam … What's the matter?
SHALE:	Why the big parade?
SAM:	You haven't heard …? It's Mr Hartington … he's dead.

There is a pause.

LOUIS:	He's – he's what …?
MARKHAM:	Did you say …?
SAM:	That's right … he's dead.
DORIS:	D – Dead …?
MARGARET:	(*With a forced laugh*) You're – you're joking!
SAM:	No … no, it's pretty serious.
MARKHAM:	(*Staggered*) Pretty serious!!!
SHALE:	My God!!!
MARGARET:	But … but … when did this happen?
DORIS:	(*Bewildered*) Hartington … dead? I – I don't believe it!
SAM:	Listen, lady! Don't try any funny business … The name's Levinsky not Harpo Marx … I say the guy's dead … all right he's dead … he's stone cold.
DORIS:	But …
LOUIS:	(*Seriously*) O.K., Sam. Who's in charge?
SAM:	Divisional-Inspector O'Hara, he's from Los Angeles. I think perhaps he'd like to see you film people. There's an entrance over on the other side of …
LOUIS:	Yes … Yes … O.K., Sam! Jump on the running board!!!

FADE IN the car moving away.
Slow FADE of scene.

FADE IN the voice of DIVISIONAL-INSPECTOR O'HARA. There are several people talking, rather excitedly, in the background.

O'HARA: Now there's got to be no slip-up on this, doc! You understand?

DOCTOR: (*Quietly*) I can only recap what I have already told you, Inspector. Mr Hartington died from poisoning ... Cyanide poisoning. There is however no trace of any other form of poison for that matter in – er – what remains of the meal.

O'HARA: H'm. What time was it when Hartington arrived here?

LOUIS: I should say it must have been ...

O'HARA: I'm not talking to you! I'll deal with you film people later!

LOUIS: (*Indignantly*) Look here ... my name's Cheyne ... Louis Cheyne ... I'm not in the habit of being insulted.

O'HARA: You'll kinda get used to it, brother!

MARGARET: What's all this nonsense about Mr Hartington being murdered? It's quite obvious he died from heart failure, so I ...

O'HARA: Oliver Hartington was murdered, lady! He was poisoned! Poisoned with cyanide. Now, if (*Raising his voice*) we can get a little peace and quiet around here, I'd like to get things straightened out!

The background of chatter dies down.

O'HARA: Now! Who are you?

SHALE: (*Quietly*) My name is Shale, Dallas Shale. I'm a scenario writer under contract to H.G.T. This is Mr Markham, one of our directors ... Miss Margaret Freeman, the actress ... Mr Louis Cheyne, a colleague of mine ... and Miss

	Charleston, Mr Hartington's confidential secretary ... oh, and this is a Miss Howard.
O'HARA:	H'm. Now where's the waiter who served Hartington?
MOORE:	I rather think that's the young man ... over there.
O'HARA:	(*Calling*) Hi! Hi, you!!!

A slight pause.

| O'HARA: | Are you the waiter that served Mr Hartington? |

The young man is an Englishman. He is very well spoken.

WAITER:	Yes. Yes, I served Mr Hartington.
O'HARA:	What time did he arrive here?
WAITER:	I should say about half past eleven.
O'HARA:	Was he alone all the time?
WAITER:	Yes. Yes, all the time.
O'HARA:	Say, you're not an American are you?
WAITER:	No, Inspector, I'm an Englishman.
O'HARA:	How long have you been over here?
WAITER:	What do you mean ... 'over here'?
O'HARA:	You know what I mean!
WAITER:	I have been in the United States of America for two years, in the State of California for six months, and employed at The Blue Stetson restaurant for precisely sixty-four days. My age is thirty-two, my height is five feet eleven, I have blue eyes, and I am passionately fond of pineapple fritters.
O'HARA:	(*Staggered*) Say ... are you trying to be funny?
WAITER:	Not in the slightest.
O'HARA:	Then ... who the hell are you anyway?
WAITER:	My name is London. Peter London.

There is yet another gasp of astonishment from the film crowd, but once again the familiar music surges in: as it slowly fades we hear the voice of CAMPBELL MANSFIELD.

MANSFIELD: (*Bewildered*) But – but I thought you said that …
girl … Gail Howard was … was … Peter
London?

SHALE: (*Chuckling: highly amused*) Some story, eh?
(*Suddenly*) Holy mackerel, is that clock right,
Charlie?

CHARLIE: Not far out, Mr Shale.

SHALE: Chee – I'd better be moving.

MANSFIELD: But – but you can't leave like this! I mean …
what … what happened next?

SHALE: (*Amused*) I'm afraid I can't go into that right
now … (*Seriously*) But … supposing you meet
me here next week, Mr Mansfield … same time
… same place?

MANSFIELD: Yes … yes … by all means.

SHALE: O.K! O.K. … That's a date. (*Suddenly*) Oh, by
the way … there's one point I forgot to mention.
You remember that cable for Hartington … the
one the Western Union boy brought to The Blue
Stetson?

MANSFIELD: Yes.

SHALE: Well, when I realised what had happened to
Hartington I sort of made myself responsible for
it. (*After a pause*) And do you know what the
cable said?

MANSFIELD: I – I can't imagine.

SHALE: It said – "Have just received news from
publishers. Will arrive Hollywood 2.30 plane
Thursday".

MANSFIELD: (*Puzzled*) Arrive Hollywood 2.30 plane
Thursday? I don't understand!

SHALE: (*Quietly*) It was sent from a small town near
Indianapolis.

MANSFIELD: Yes, but – but who sent it?

25

SHALE: Well, the name on the cable was ... Peter
                London.
MANSFIELD: (*Staggered*) Peter ... London ...?
SHALE: Yeah ... Peter London. See you next week, Mr
                Mansfield. Same time. Same place. Goodnight,
                Charlie.

It is now nine o'clock and the cuckoo clock announces the fact.

                Cuckoo! Cuckoo! Cuckoo! Cuckoo! Cuckoo!
                Cuckoo! Cuckoo! Cuckoo! Cuckoo!

*The second clock commences to chime, but the familiar music
FADES IN.*

END OF EPISODE ONE

EPISODE TWO

WHO IS PETER LONDON?

OPEN TO: Cuckoo! Cuckoo! Cuckoo! Cuckoo!
          Cuckoo! Cuckoo! Cuckoo! Cuckoo!

A second clock chimes the hour.
DALLAS SHALE arrives ... he is slightly out of breath.

SHALE: Hello ... Hello, there! Am I ... am I late?

MANSFIELD: No ... No, rather not. I've ordered you a highball.

SHALE: Oh, swell! (*Making himself comfortable*) Well, how are you liking Hollywood, Mr Mansfield?

MANSFIELD: I'm liking Hollywood fine; but you were – er – telling me the story of ...

SHALE: Oh, yes! Now let's see ... where did I get to? ... with the story, I mean.

MANSFIELD: Well, you told me that Oliver Hartington ... (*With a laugh*) ... in other words the Czar of Hollywood ... endeavoured to find a young novelist by the name of Peter London because he – that is Hartington – wanted to buy the film rights of Peter London's novel The Modern Pilgrim.

SHALE: That's right. And one day, after Hartington had left for The Blue Stetson restaurant, a young girl had appeared at the studio by the name of Gail Howard and ...

MANSFIELD: And she said that ... she was Peter London ...

SHALE: (*Amused*) Correct! Anyway, we ... that is Julius Markham, the producer ... Louis Cheyne, the writer ... Margaret Freeman, the actress ... and Doris Charleston ...

MANSFIELD: Hartington's secretary ...?

SHALE: Yeah ... all dashed down to The Blue Stetson restaurant: taking with us, of course, this girl ... er ... Gail Howard.

| MANSFIELD: | And don't forget the cable you received – the one for Hartington ... the one the boy gave you outside of the restaurant. |
| SHALE: | Oh, yeah! Yeah, that's right – I pushed it into my pocket. Anyway, when we arrived at The Blue Stetson Hartington had already been murdered and Divisional-Inspector O'Hara was in charge of the proceedings. He was a rather quick tempered little man with ... |

FADE VOICE.

FADE IN the scene at The Blue Stetson.
There is a great deal of animated conversation taking place.

| O'HARA: | Oliver Hartington was murdered, lady! He was poisoned! Poisoned with cyanide. Now, if (*Raising his voice*) we can get a little peace and quiet around here, I'd like to get things straightened out! |

The background of chatter dies down.
There is a slight pause.

O'HARA:	Now! Who are you?
SHALE:	(*Quietly*) My name is Shale, Dallas Shale. I'm a scenario writer under contract to H.G.T. This is Mr Markham, one of our directors ... Miss Margaret Freeman, the actress ... Mr Louis Cheyne, a colleague of mine ... and Miss Charleston, Mr Hartington's confidential secretary ... oh, and this is a Miss Howard.
O'HARA:	M'm. Now where's the waiter who served Hartington?
MOORE:	I rather think that's the young man ... over there.
O'HARA:	(*Calling*) Hi! Hi, you!!!

A slight pause.

O'HARA: Are you the waiter that served Mr Hartington?

The young man is an Englishman. He is very well spoken.

PETER: Yes. Yes, I served Mr Hartington.

O'HARA: What time did he arrive here?

PETER: I should say about half past eleven.

O'HARA: Was he alone all the time?

PETER: Yes. Yes, all the time.

O'HARA: Say, you're not an American are you?

PETER: No, Inspector, I'm an Englishman.

O'HARA: How long have you been over here?

PETER: What do you mean ... 'over here'?

O'HARA: You know what I mean!

PETER: I have been in the United States of America for two years, in the State of California for six months, and employed at The Blue Stetson restaurant for precisely sixty-four days. My age is thirty-two, my height is five feet eleven, I have blue eyes, and I am passionately fond of pineapple fritters.

O'HARA: (*Staggered*) Say ... are you trying to be funny?

PETER: Not in the slightest.

O'HARA: Then ... who the hell are you anyway?

PETER: My name is London. Peter London.

There is yet another gasp of astonishment.

MARKHAM: Peter ... London!!!

O'HARA: Say, you're ... you're not the guy Hartington was looking for? Not this author Johnny all the newspapers have been squawking about?

PETER: If, by that you mean: did I write a book called The Modern Pilgrim? The answer is ... yes.

O'HARA: Then why, in heaven's name, didn't you shout up about it? For six solid weeks the whole of America has had to listen to a lot of ballyhoo

31

	about an elusive author by the name of Peter London; and here, right under their very…
LOUIS:	Just a minute! Just a minute, Inspector! <u>This</u> young lady claims to be Peter London.
O'HARA:	What!!!
GAIL:	(*Alarmed*) No! No, there's some mistake I … I …
MARKHAM:	(*Indignantly*) Some mistake? You came to the studio this evening and told us that you were the author of The Modern Pilgrim – that you'd written it under the pseudonym of Peter London.
DORIS:	Yes. Yes, of course you did!
MARGARET:	If you aren't Peter London, then … who are you?
GAIL:	My name is Gail Howard … I'm – I'm an actress. I said that I was Peter London so that I could …
MARKHAM:	Oh, my God!
SHALE:	(*Quietly; but significantly*) I say, just a minute!
A tiny pause.	
LOUIS:	What is it?
DORIS:	What are you reading?
SHALE:	This cable … it came for Hartington just after we left the office, and …
O'HARA:	I'll take care of that!
MARGARET:	Where's it from?
SHALE:	(*Thoughtfully*) Indiana.
LOUIS:	(*Quietly*) What is it, Shale?
O'HARA:	(*Staggered*) Say, what the hell's the meaning of this?
MARKHAM:	(*Irritatedly*) Since we haven't seen the cable, Inspector, I fail to see …

32

O'HARA:	It's from a small town near Indianapolis, Mr Markham, and it says: (*Reading*) "Have just received news from publishers. Will arrive Hollywood 2.30 plane Thursday … Peter London".
MARKHAM:	Peter London!!!
PETER:	Peter … London!!!
O'HARA:	Yeah … Peter London!!! (*Exasperated*) Now what the hell is going on around here?
PETER:	(*Calmly*) A little while ago I told you that I was Peter London, the author of that extremely tiresome book The Modern Pilgrim, and since I am not in the habit of lying – even to members of the Californian Constabulary – I can assure you that I am … Peter London.
O'HARA:	Californian cons … (*Bellowing*) Sergeant!
MOORE:	Yes, sir?
O'HARA:	Get this guy down to headquarters!
MOORE:	Yes, sir.
O'HARA:	And the girl!!!
GAIL:	(*Alarmed*) Look here, Inspector, you … can't take me down to police headquarters just because …
O'HARA:	That's your guess sister! (*Turning*) I want all you people back at Hartington's office!
LOUIS:	(*Irritated*) What now?
O'HARA:	Yeah … now! I'm going through that office from top to bottom, and I want all you film people on tap.
MARKHAM:	(*Sarcastically*) What do you expect to find, Inspector … Hedy Lamarr?
O'HARA:	I expect to find a motive, Mr Markham … catch on?

FADE IN music.

FADE DOWN music.

FADE IN a motor car. It is travelling fairly fast. The boulevard is crowded; there is a great deal of traffic.

MOORE: Say, slow down, Ed!

ED: Nervous?

MOORE: No, I'm not nervous, but it's kinda skiddy.

A slight pause.

PETER: Do you mind if I smoke?

MOORE: Go ahead.

PETER: (*Offering GAIL a cigarette*) Miss ... Howard? (*Politely*) It – er – is Miss Howard?

GAIL: No, thank you.

PETER: Sergeant?

MOORE: Oh ... er ... thanks ...

The horn is heard ... a sudden warning to a careless pedestrian.

ED: (*Shouting; annoyed*) Look where you're going you ... you ... (*Exasperated*) Oh, chee!

MOORE: Keep your eyes in front, Ed!

ED: But did you see that guy?

MOORE: Yeah ... yeah, I saw him ... but take it easy!

ED: (*Grumbling*) That's o.k. ... but I've got a date at twelve.

MOORE: Date or no date you've got to drive me back to The Blue Stetson ... (*Suddenly*) Say, what sort of a date is this anyway? Twelve o'clock at night is no time for a respectable ...

GAIL: (*Excitedly*) Look at that car!!!!

PETER: He's skidding!!!

MOORE: (*Shouting*) Look out, Ed!!! Look out!!! (*Angrily*) Do something you crazy loon!!!

ED: (*Bewildered*) What – what the hell can I do?

PETER: (*Quietly; urgently*) Get your head down!

GAIL: But ... but ...

PETER: Get your head down!!!

The two cars crash. There is a babble of excited voices. A motor horn is heard.

GAIL: Are … are you all right?

PETER: Yes …

ED: (*Shouting*) Why the hell didn't you straighten up?

2nd DRIVER: (*From the background*) If you'd used your brains this wouldn't have happened!!!

ED: (*Staggered*) Why, you …

MOORE: (*Taking command*) That's O.K. I'll handle this guy!

The car door slams.

PETER: Did the smash frighten you?

GAIL: No. No, I'm all right.

PETER: Good.

In the background: voices are raised in anger and annoyance.

ED: This would happen! I guess we'll be here all night. (*Exasperated again*) Oh, chee!

PETER: (*Softly: tensely*) Listen … do you know this boulevard well?

GAIL: Yes. Yes, I think so … Why? (*Suddenly*) Why do you ask?

PETER: (*Quietly*) There's no reason why we shouldn't make a dash for it, you know.

GAIL: (*With a little laugh*) Oh, we'd … we'd never get away … why … why … (*She is thinking about it*)

PETER: Are you … 'game' …?

GAIL: Yes, but …

PETER: (*Quickly*) About a hundred yards down, on the right-hand side, there's a fun-fair palace, do you know the place I mean?

GAIL: I think so. It's opposite Wong's arcade …

PETER: That's the place! Make straight for the main entrance. Just inside the door you'll see a wax model of Joan Crawford ... I'll meet you there. (*After a tiny pause*) All right?

GAIL: (*Softly*) All right ...

A pause.

PETER: (*A whisper*) Good luck!

The car door closes.

ED: (*Suddenly*) Hello! Say, what the hell does she think ...

PETER brings his fist forward.

ED: Ow!!! (*He falls across the seat*)

PETER: Awfully sorry, old boy ... had to be done!

The car door opens and slams.

FADE UP a background of angry voices.

MOORE: Now listen, it's no good you trying to tell me what happened because I was in the car!

2nd DRIVER: I don't care a damn whether you were in the car or not; I still maintain that if your driver had ... (*Puzzled*) What is it?

MOORE: (*Suddenly galvanized into action*) Stop that man! Stop that man! Oh, my God!

There is general pandemonium. Motor car horns. Police whistles.

MOORE: Stop him!!! Let me get through here!!! For God's sake let me get through!!! Stop that man!!! Ed!!! Ed ... Where the hell are you? Stop that man!!! Stop ... him!!!

FADE DOWN on scene.

FADE SCENE completely.

FADE IN of mechanical funfair music and a background of voices. There is a certain amount of ribald laughter. Numerous barkers can be heard.

PETER arrives. He is almost out of breath.

PETER: So ... so ... you made it! G...good!

GAIL:	What happened?
PETER:	(*Quickly*) Let's get inside …
GAIL:	Did he see you?
PETER:	Yes, I'm afraid the Sergeant spotted me … He's – he's not far behind!
GAIL:	Isn't it rather unwise to go in here? I mean, if there's only one entrance …
PETER:	We've got no choice, unless … (*Suddenly*) There he is! Come on! Be quick!
GAIL:	Where – where are we going?
PETER:	Quickly!!!

FADE UP of the funfair music and background noises.

PETER and GAIL are pushing headlong through the crowd.

1st BARKER: Step right this way! Right this way, my good people … for the greatest entertainment of all time … see for yourselves, in graphic detail, one might almost say in pornographic detail! – how your favourite film stars spend their leisure moments … for example, that celebrated young … (*Aside*) Take it easy, sir! Take it easy … No stampeding, if you please … (*Continuing*) For example, that celebrated … (*FADE voice*)

GAIL:	(*Bewildered*) Where – where are we going?
PETER:	I – I … think we'd better try and lose him in this crowd, otherwise …
GAIL:	He can still see us …
PETER:	Yes … don't worry, we'll shake him off … stick close …

FADE IN of oriental music, together with the voice of the 2nd BARKER.

2nd BARKER: Introducing Princess Kenzeno! One of the most glamorous, and at the same time one of the most fascinating personalities of today. The Princess has had the rare, one might almost venture to say the unique experience of sharing the intimate secrets of European society. This evening, for the very first time, we have persuaded ... (*FADE AWAY from voice*)

FADE IN train effects ... an obvious recording of train whistle, engine letting off steam etc. There is a certain amount of excited laughter.

3rd BARKER: This is it! This is it, folks! The one and only Ghost Train! Take your seats, if you please! (*Aside*) Get your tickets at the box, buddy! (*Continuing*) Step this way, folks!!! The thrill of a lifetime!! Clark Gable's favourite sideshow ... the one and only Ghost Train!!! (*Aside*) Don't get so excited, buddy, there's plenty of room!! (*Continuing*) We positively guarantee this to be the greatest spine-chiller of the century ... Step this way for the Ghost Train ...!!!

FADE IN PETER and GAIL.

PETER: (*Breathlessly*) Are – are you all right?

GAIL: Yes ... but ... but I don't think I can ... I can keep this up!

PETER: (*Laughing*) Don't worry!

3rd BARKER: Step this way for the Ghost Train!! The thrill of a lifetime!!! This way for Clark Gable's favourite sideshow ... the one and only Ghost Train!!!

GAIL: (*Surprised*) I say, we're ... not going in here?

PETER: Don't worry, I know what I'm doing ... (*Aside*) Two please ... thanks ...

A small turnstile clicks open. There is a sudden rush of air and several hysterical screams ... a 'train' arrives and disgorges a crowd of excited people.

3rd BARKER: Take your seats, please! Take your seats for ... the Ghost Train!!!

PETER: Get in here ... Quickly!!!

GAIL: (*With a sigh of relief*) Oh!! Well ... I'm certainly glad
            to ... get ... get ... sat ... (*She is out of breath*)
PETER: (*Suddenly*) Keep down!!!
GAIL: What's the matter?
PETER: The Sergeant ... he's stood near the entrance ...
            (*Anxiously*) I wish to God this would start ...

*There is a sudden shrill whistle ... the carriages move forward ...
there are several nervous and excited voices ...*

GAIL: We're off!!!
PETER: Yes ... I don't think he spotted us!
GAIL: (*Laughing; having recovered her breath*) What is this
            thing ...? What happens?
PETER: (*Imitating the BARKER*) Clark Gable's favourite
            sideshow! The one and only Ghost Train ...
GAIL: (*Amused*) Idiot! (*Seriously*) I do hope the Sergeant
            didn't notice us! We're in a tight corner if he did,
            because he's only got to wait by ...
PETER: (*Interrupting GAIL*) This gives us time to think
            anyway.

*The carriages enter a tunnel ... there are several nervous laughs
... a great deal of excitement ... Suddenly, in the background a
wild hysterical laugh is heard ...*

GAIL: (*Suddenly*) Look! Look! ... There's a skeleton!
PETER: (*Laughing*) It's all right ... it's only a dummy!

The wild hysterical laughter is repeated.

GAIL: (*Quickly: alarmed*) Something touched my face!
PETER: There's nothing to get worried about ... it's only wet
            string ...
A GIRL: Now stop that, wise guy!

A slap is heard.

A MAN: Ah'm sorry, honey ...

A tiny pause.

GAIL: (*Suddenly*) What's that? What that in front? Why ...
            why, it's a lion!!

A lion is heard ... wild and ferocious.

PETER: (*Amused*) That's clever!!! (*He laughs*)

The lion roars.

A NEGRO: Boy ... oh, boy ... ah'm sure is terrified!!!!

Suddenly a whistle is heard ... loud and terrifying ... it makes everyone jump.

A WOMAN: My God, this is awful!!!

A voice booms out from the background ... a loud, horrific voice.

VOICE: Keep your heads down! Keep your heads down! Keep your heads down!

The VOICE draws nearer.

VOICE: Keep your heads down! Keep your heads down!

The VOICE fades away.

VOICE: Keep your heads down! Keep your heads down! Keep your heads down! Keep your heads down!

The VOICE FADES completely.

GAIL: (*With a sigh of relief*) Oh!

NEGRO: Boy ... Oh, boy! ... Ah'm sure is terrified!!

There is a little laughter.

Another VOICE booms from the background ... A WOMAN's VOICE ... sinister ... and demoniacal ...

WOMAN'S VOICE: Welcome strangers! You are approaching the valley of a thousand ghosts ...

Music is heard ... strange, spookish music ...

WOMAN: Say, I can't stand this ... I'm getting the hell out of here!!!

MAN: Stay where you are, sugar! You'll be O.K.!!!

WOMAN: I'll certainly need beauty treatment after this ride!!!

NEGRO: Boy ... oh, boy! ... ah'm sure is terrified!!!

A slight pause.

PETER: (*Quietly*) The ride won't last much longer: we'd better start making arrangements.

GAIL: (*Almost a whisper*) Suppose he's waiting for us?

PETER:	I don't think he will be, but we can't take any chances. (*Tensely*) Now listen! When this ride finishes I don't want you to leave your seat … Sit tight and go round for a second time!
GAIL:	Oh, not again … please!
PETER:	It's our only chance. I'll leave the booth and make a dash for it. If the old boy is waiting for us, that ought to draw him away, for a time at any rate. (*Thoughtfully*) You know, he never actually saw you enter the funfair, so he might even get the impression I'm on my own.
GAIL:	(*Reluctantly*) Yes, but … I shan't know what happens, and …
PETER:	Oh, yes, you will! Do you know an apartment house called Sante Barbara, it's about a hundred yards past The Garden of Allah?
GAIL:	Yes. Yes, I … think so.
PETER:	Well, a friend of mine has an apartment; in the Sante Barbara building, I mean. He's out of town at the moment and I'm using his flat. Supposing … supposing we arrange to meet there … that is … if we both make it o.k.?
GAIL:	Yes. Yes, all right.
PETER:	Good. It's flat 14 on the sixth floor … the name is Wendleford … Mike Wendleford. Can you remember that?
GAIL:	Yes. Yes, I think so … Sante Barbara building … Flat 14 … Sixth floor … Mike Wendleford …
PETER:	That's it! (*Softly, urgently*) We're coming out into the open …

FADE IN the voice of the 3rd BARKER.

3rd BARKER:	This is it, folks! The one and only Ghost Train! Clark Gable's favourite sideshow! The thrill of the year! The spine-chiller of the century!!!

The carriages draw to a standstill; the excited, nervous, amused, and frightened passengers alight.

PETER: Goodbye! Sit tight!

GAIL: I've got my fingers crossed!

PETER: If the Sergeant's in sight, don't worry … I'll entice him away …

GAIL: (*Amused*) Good luck!

3rd BARKER: Roll up boys and gals for the greatest thrill of all time!!! Take your seats for the one and only Ghost Train!!!

FADE IN of the train effects.

3rd BARKER: This is it! This is it, folks!!! The greatest thrill on earth … Take your seats, if you please!!! Clark Gable's favourite sideshow!!! The thrill sensation of the century … The super-special … (*Suddenly; aside*) Take it easy, sugar!!! Take it easy!!! (*Continuing*) Here we are folks!!! Here we are!!! The one and only Ghost Train!!!

The train effects are heard followed by a babble of excited voices. Suddenly the Sergeant's voice is heard … he is wildly excited.

MOORE: Stop him!!! Stop that man!!! Stop that man!!! For God's sake get out of the way!!! Stop that!!! Get out of the way!!! Get out … of … the … blasted … way!!!

3rd BARKER: My! Oh, my!! Naughty!!! Naughty!!! (*Continuing*) Roll up boys and gals … Roll up!!! The greatest thrill of all time!!! The spinechiller of the century!!! The super-special … (*Suddenly: aside*) Take it easy, sugar!!! Take it easy!!!

FADE IN of train effects … excited voices … general laughter … and the weary, desperate voice of SERGEANT MOORE.

MOORE: Stop him!!! Stop … that … man!!! Stop … that … man!!! Stop … that … man … (*FADE voice*)

FADE from the scene to the insistent ringing of a telephone.

O'HARA: (*Briskly*) That's o.k., I'll take it!!! (*He lifts the receiver*) Hello ...? ... Yeah, this is Hartington's office ... no, this is Divisional-Inspector O'Hara ... Who is that? (*Aside*) It's a guy called Webb ... He's talking from 'Frisco.

DORIS: All right, I'll take it! (*On the phone*) Hello ... is that you, Fred? ... Yes, this is Doris ... M'm? ... Oh, yes ... Yes, it's quite true ... About an hour ago ... Well ... They seem to think it's murder ... Search me ... Yes ... Yes, I'll tell Markham ... Goodbye! (*She replaces the receiver*)

O'HARA: Who was that guy?

DORIS: Just one of the boys. He'd heard a rumour about Hartington and wanted to know if there was any truth in it.

O'HARA: M'm. (*He is searching the desk*) How long have you been here?

DORIS: In Hollywood?

O'HARA: No. No ... working for Hartington?

DORIS: Nine years.

O'HARA: Did you like him?

DORIS: Oh, he was a sweet, simple, benevolent old gentleman.

O'HARA: Yeah! Where's the key to this drawer?

DORIS: In front of you.

O'HARA: Oh! (*He takes the key and opens the drawer*) M'm ... (*To himself*) Cheque book ... cigarette case ... dice ... fountain pen ... Say, what's this?

DORIS: It looks like a contract of some sort.

O'HARA: (*Reading*) "Memorandum of Agreement made this twenty-third day of August one thousand nine hundred and thirty-two between Peter London

43

(hereinafter called the author) of the one part and Norman Roger Page (hereinafter called the agent) of the other part. Whereas it is agreed that for the sum of fifty pounds (receipt whereof the author hereby acknowledges) the author sells outright to the agent all the film, dramatic, and publication rights of the novel written by him and entitled: The Modern Pilgrim ..." (*Puzzled*) I don't get this! This contract means that Hartington <u>had</u> the film rights of The Modern Pilgrim ... Look! Look, it's made over to him ... (*Reading*) "All rights transferred to Oliver Hartington ... signed: Norman Roger Page" ... (*Bewildered*) If Hartington already had the film rights ... what the hell was all the ballyhoo about? The newspapers said that he wanted to contact Peter London in order to buy the film rights of his novel ... but – but the crazy loon had already got 'em ... he'd got all the rights!!!

DORIS: (*Quietly*) Let me see that agreement.

O'HARA: Say, who's this guy ... Norman Roger Page? D'you know him?

DORIS: (*Thoughtfully*) No. He's certainly not one of the well-known agents ...

O'HARA: (*Slowly*) Did you ... know about this agreement?

DORIS: No. No, it's ... news to me, I must say.

There is a knock on the door and Mary Brampton enters.

MARY: Oh! Oh, I'm sorry, Miss Charleston.

DORIS: That's all right! Come in, Mary!

O'HARA: Who is this?

DORIS: Mary Brampton ... she's Markham's secretary. Oh, Mary ... this is Chief-Ins ...

O'HARA: Divisional-Inspector ...

DORIS: Divisional-Inspector O'Hara.

MARY: How – do – you – do, Inspector?

44

O'HARA: You girls seem to work kinda late around here.

MARY: I'm just leaving. I shan't be in till Tuesday, Miss Charleston, so I thought ... (*She hesitates*) I say, I'm most awfully sorry ... about Mr Hartington ... (*Puzzled*) But ... what happened?

O'HARA: Did you ever work for Hartington?

MARY: Only for about a fortnight. Miss Charleston was ill and ...

O'HARA: When was that?

MARY: Oh, about ... four or five weeks ago.

O'HARA: M'm ... take a look at this.

MARY: What is it?

O'HARA: It's an agreement ... read it!

A pause.

MARY: But – but this means that Mr Hartington actually had the film rights of The Modern Pilgrim.

O'HARA: Smart girl!

MARY: Then ... what was all the fuss about? He had practically everybody in America searching for Peter London, because he wanted to buy the film rights, and yet ... and yet ... he'd got them all the time. (*Puzzled*) That doesn't make sense.

O'HARA: You said it, lady! Anyhow, the point, so far as I'm concerned, is this ... Have you seen that agreement before?

MARY: No.

O'HARA: You've no idea who he got it from?

DORIS: Obviously the agent ... Norman Roger Page.

O'HARA: Yeah, but who is ... Norman Roger Page? The name's a phoney if you ask me.

The door opens and SERGEANT QUINN enters.

O'HARA: What is it, Sergeant?

In the background, through the half open door voices are heard.

QUINN: Say, Inspector, these people are getting restless. There's a guy out here talking plenty powerful.

O'HARA: What's his name?

QUINN: Markham.

O'HARA: Well, you can present my compliments to Mr Julius Markham, Sergeant, and you can tell him – and the rest of the chromium plated riff-raff – that I shall have the dubious pleasure of their company in about thirty seconds.

QUINN: Yes, sir.

The door closes.

O'HARA: O.K. ... Miss Brampton, you needn't wait.

MARY: Oh ... er ... goodnight, Miss Charleston.

A second door opens and closes.

DORIS: (*Coldly: indignantly*) I'm quite well aware that this is neither the time nor the place to give vent to one's personal feelings, but you are – without exception – the rudest and the most insulting individual that it has ever been my misfortune to ...

O'HARA: (*Quietly interrupting DORIS: he is reading for the counterfoils of a cheque book*) "Doris Charleston ... May 9th, 1940 ... Five hundred dollars ... D.C. ... April 7th, 1940 ... Six hundred dollars ... D.C. ... June 3rd, 1940 ... Three hundred dollars ... Doris Charleston ... July 8th, 1940 ... Eight hundred dollars ..."

DORIS: (*Softly*) What – what is that?

O'HARA: It's the counterfoil of a cheque book, Miss Charleston ... Mr Hartington's cheque book ... makes interesting reading ...

DORIS: (*Nervously: uncertain of herself*) I ... I used to help Mr Hartington occasionally with ... with ... with creative work, and he ... he was very generous.

O'HARA: Yeah …? Hello, this is interesting … (*Reading*) "August 4ᵗʰ, 1940 … D.C. … nine hundred dollars … and for the last time" … Now what did Mr Hartington mean by that … "and for the last time"…?

DORIS: (*Almost frightened*) I … I don't know.

O'HARA: No? (*Pleasantly*) O.K. … Let's see what's biting our dear Julius.

The door opens and a babble of conversations is heard. MARGARET FREEMAN, JULIUS MARKHAM, LOUIS CHEYNE, DALLAS SHALE, and SERGEANT QUINN …

MARKHAM: For God's sake!!! Are we to stick here all night arguing ourselves hoarse just …

The conversation dies down on O'HARA's entrance.

O'HARA: You were saying, Mr Markham?

MARKHAM: Oh! Oh, so here you are … at last. What the devil's been going on in that office?

MARGARET: We've been here hours!

O'HARA: You've been here exactly forty-five minutes … and a very interesting forty-five minutes, Miss Freeman. (*Suddenly*) Have any of you celebrities heard of a guy called Norman Roger Page?

LOUIS: (*Puzzled*) Norman Roger Page?

SHALE: What is he … an actor?

O'HARA: No. I reckon he's some sort of an agent … maybe. Take a look at this … It's a contract … it was in Hartington's desk …

There is a pause.

They are all rather astonished by the agreement.

MARKHAM: But – but this is crazy!!!!

LOUIS: I don't understand this, at all!!!

MARGARET: (*Staggered*) That's – that's the very thing that Hartington wanted!!!

47

SHALE:	He was dead set on buying the film rights of The Modern Pilgrim, why ... why he'd every agent in America looking for Peter London so that he could clinch the deal.
DORIS:	(*Quietly*) No. No, that's isn't quite true.
SHALE:	What do you mean, Doris?
MARKHAM:	(*Staggered*) What the hell d'you mean ... it isn't quite true ...?
DORIS:	I mean that Hartington wasn't interested in the film rights of The Modern Pilgrim.
MARKHAM:	Then what was he interested in?

A tiny pause.

DORIS:	Peter London.
LOUIS:	(*Surprised*) Peter London ...?
MARGARET:	(*Puzzled*) I don't get this?
DORIS:	Six weeks ago, Mr Hartington made up his mind to make one or two rather dramatic changes in the ... shall we say? ... studio personnel. It was his intention, for instance, to get rid of certain members of the story department. About this time Hartington bought a book at a second-hand stall ... it was The Modern Pilgrim by Peter London. He read the book, and he liked it, and he made up his mind that he was going to bring the author to Hollywood and put him in complete charge of the H.G.T. scenario departments.
LOUIS:	What!!!
MARKHAM:	Are you crazy?
SHALE:	(*Chuckling*) Gee ... that was just like Hartington.
O'HARA:	Go on, Miss Charleston ...
DORIS:	Hartington knew of course that the suggestion would meet with a certain amount of opposition; so he made up his mind that, first of all, the best thing to do was to let everyone think he was

merely interested in the film rights of the novel. But no one could find Peter London ... even to buy the film rights. No one in fact had ever heard of Peter London!!! And did this make Hartington see red? And how! But not because he wanted the film rights ... Oh, no! ... But because he wanted Peter London. Peter London himself ... here ... in Hollywood!

LOUIS: Well ... well, I'm damned!

MARKHAM: Say, are you sure about this?

DORIS: Absolutely.

SHALE: (*Almost to himself*) And all the time Peter London was here ... right under his very nose ... at The Blue Stetson ...

MARKHAM: Just a minute! We're not sure that guy is Peter London ... Don't forget the cable from Indianapolis!

MARGARET: I still don't see the point about the contract?

O'HARA: Someone must have sold this contract to Hartington, or at least attempted to sell it to him, firmly believing that the only thing that interested Hartington was the film rights of the novel! Now it seems to me ...

O'HARA is interrupted by the telephone ringing.

DORIS: O'Hara? ... Yes ... Yes, he's here ... Who is that, please? (*To O'HARA*) It's Sergeant Moore ...

O'HARA: Sergeant Moore? (*Taking the receiver*) Hello ... Yeah ... (*Staggered*) What!!! Why ... why you crazy guy!!! (*Angrily*) Don't talk back you dumb cluck ... Get a radio flash out ... Yeah ... Yeah ... Quick!!! (*He replaces the receiver*) God-damn-it!

DORIS: What is it?

49

O'HARA: It's that girl ... and the waiter ... they've – they've made a dash for it!!!

FADE IN music which is quick and dramatic.

CROSSFADE to the sound of police sirens ... followed by police cars ... and the motorcycle police.

FADE to background for –

1st VOICE: Calling all cars! Calling all cars! Calling all cars! Calling all cars! Calling all cars! Calling all cars! Calling all ... (*FADE OVER 2nd VOICE*)

2nd VOICE: ... last seen near Wong's Arcade, Vine Street ... Height about five feet four ... brunette ... wearing a dark brown costume and ... (*FADE OVER to 3rd VOICE*)

3rd VOICE: ... Be on the lookout for Peter London ... Peter London ... Height about five feet eleven ... dressed in a white tuxedo and wearing a black and white ... (*FADE OVER to 4th VOICE*)

4th VOICE: Calling all cars! Calling all cars! Be on the lookout for Peter London and Gail Howard ... Calling all cars! Calling all cars! (*FADE to 2nd VOICE*)

2nd VOICE: ... last seen near Wong's Arcade, Vine Street ... Height about five feet four ... brunette ... wearing a dark brown costume and ... *(FADE OVER to 3rd VOICE)*

3rd VOICE: ... Be on the lookout for Peter London ... Peter London ... Height about five feet eleven ... dressed in a white tuxedo and wearing a black and white ... (*FADE OVER to 1st VOICE*)

1st VOICE: Calling all cars! Calling all cars! Calling all cars! Calling all cars! Calling all ... (*FADE voice*)

FADE UP the sound of police cars with sirens blaring and motorcycle police.

50

CROSSFADE to music.

Slow FADE DOWN for the voice of CAMPBELL MANSFIELD.

MANSFIELD: (*Anxiously*) But – but what happened? I mean – did the waiter and that girl … what's her name … Gail Howard … Did they actually escape or …

SHALE: Well, after the young man made a … (*Suddenly*) say, is that clock right?

CHARLIE: Yes, sir.

SHALE: Chee, I'd better be making a move! I've got an appointment down town at …

MANSFIELD: Yes … but … but what happened? I mean you – er – you can't just leave the story like this … I mean to say, it's … er … it's …

SHALE: (*Chuckling*) Well, supposing we meet here next week …?

MANSFIELD: Yes … yes, rather! By all means!

SHALE: The same time?

MANSFIELD: Yes … Yes, rather! By all means! (*With an amused, yet bewildered chuckle*) I mean to say …

The cuckoo clock announces the time.

Cuckoo! Cuckoo! Cuckoo! Cuckoo! Cuckoo! Cuckoo! Cuckoo! Cuckoo! Cuckoo!

Closing music.

END OF EPISODE TWO

EPISODE THREE

MAKINGS OF A
FILM STAR

.

OPEN TO: Cuckoo! Cuckoo! Cuckoo! Cuckoo!
                  Cuckoo! Cuckoo! Cuckoo! Cuckoo!
A second clock chimes the hour.

DALLAS SHALE arrives ... once again he is slightly out of breath.

SHALE: Hello ... Hello, there! Am I ... Am I late?

MANSFIELD: No ... No, rather not. I've ordered you a highball.

SHALE: Oh, swell! (*After a tiny pause*) Now let's see ... Where did I get to? ... With the story, I mean ...

MANSFIELD: Well, you told me that Oliver Hartington ... (*With a laugh*) ... in other words the Czar of Hollywood ... endeavoured to find a young novelist by the name of Peter London because he – that is, Hartington – wanted to buy the film rights of Peter London's novel The Modern Pilgrim.

SHALE: That's right. And one night, after Hartington has left for The Blue Stetson restaurant, a young girl appeared at the studio by the name of Gail Howard and ...

MANSFIELD: And she said that ... she was Peter London ...

SHALE: Correct! Anyway, we ... that is, Julius Markham, the producer ... Louis Cheyne, the writer ... Margaret Freeman, the actress ... and Doris Charleston – Hartington's secretary – all dashed down to The Blue Stetson. When we arrived at the restaurant, Hartington had already been murdered and Divisional-Inspector O'Hara was in charge of the proceedings. He was a rather quick-tempered little man, but he very soon discovered that the waiter who served Hartington claimed to be none other than Peter London. At

	this moment, I produced a cable for Mr Hartington ... which had just arrived ... And to our surprise, it stated that Peter London would be ...
MANSFIELD:	... arriving on the 2.30 plane from Indianapolis ... next Thursday.
SHALE:	(*Laughing*) Yeah! At this point, O'Hara lost his temper and sent Peter London – that is, the waiter – and Gail Howard down to police headquarters. On the way to police headquarters, however, they escaped and arranged to meet later in the evening at an apartment house on Lea Brea Avenue.
MANSFIELD:	Yes ... Yes, I remember that. (*Puzzled*) But tell me ... who is this girl ... Gail Howard? I mean ... where did she come from ...? What made her come to Hollywood in the first place? And why ...?
SHALE:	(*Laughing*) Forgive me laughing, but ... that's exactly what Peter London wanted to know. (*Suddenly, seriously*) Anyway, when Gail arrived at the apartment house she was surprised and also delighted ... (*Start to FADE voice*) ... to discover that ... (*FADE voice completely*)

A door opens and shuts.
GAIL HOWARD is breathless with excitement.

GAIL:	Good evening! I – I want Mr Wendleford's apartment, please.
JANITOR:	Take the elevator ... Number 14 ... Sixth floor.
GAIL:	Thank you.

A pause.

There is a knock on the door of the apartment. The knock is repeated. The door opens.

PETER: (*Delightedly*) So you made it! (*With a sigh of relief*) Oh, thank goodness for that! (*Quickly*) Come inside!

The door closes.

GAIL: What a lovely fire!

PETER: Let me take your coat ... (*Taking GAIL's coat*) Ah, that's better!

GAIL: I say, this is very nice, isn't it?

PETER: Yes ... it belongs to a friend of mine ... Mike Wendleford, he's on the camera staff at Metro. My own humble abode is a one-room flatlet on the other side of town. (*Laughing*) Just at the moment, it's probably being gaily surrounded by G-men. (*Casually*) Help yourself to coffee ...

GAIL: My word, you have been busy! How long have you been here?

PETER: Oh, about ten minutes ... I had one narrow squeak at the corner of the arcade. By the way, how did you get on?

GAIL: Not too badly; it was pretty easy going once I got out of the funfair.

PETER: Yes. (*After a slight hesitation*) I suppose no one saw you enter the elevator, when ...

GAIL: Only the janitor; I asked him which floor the apartment was on. (*A tiny pause*) Why?

PETER: Well – it seems there's a girl called Mary Brampton; she works for Hartington ... I only discovered it this evening but apparently she lives here ... she has an apartment on the tenth floor.

GAIL: I see.

There is a pause.

PETER: What are you thinking about?

GAIL: I was just wondering ... who killed Mr Hartington?

57

PETER: (*Quietly*) Is that all … you were thinking about?

GAIL: (*After a pause*) No. (*Suddenly*) Your name is Peter London, isn't it?

PETER: Yes.

GAIL: And you did write the book … The Modern Pilgrim?

PETER: (*Faintly amused*) Yes … I did write The Modern Pilgrim. (*After a tiny pause*) Why, don't you believe me?

GAIL: Oh, yes! Yes, I believe you, but …

PETER: But … what …?

GAIL: Well, there's that cable, you know … the one that Inspector O'Hara read … it said …

PETER: It said: "Have just received news from publishers. Will arrive Hollywood 2.30 plane Thursday … Peter London."

GAIL: Yes. (*A slight pause*) Who do you think … sent that cable?

PETER: Well, it's rather difficult to say, isn't it? I only know who didn't send it … Peter London. (*After a slight pause*) Forgive me asking, but how long have you been in Hollywood?

GAIL: About twelve months.

PETER: What made you come here?

GAIL: I was offered a contract …

PETER: A contract …?

GAIL: Yes … with H.G.T.….

PETER: (*Surprised*) Did they see you in a play or something?

GAIL: They saw me in a bathing costume.

PETER: (*Amused*) In a bathing costume!

GAIL: Yes. I won a beauty competition. (*Laughing*) Well, don't look so surprised … please!

58

PETER: (*Laughing*) I'm sorry but ... well ... apart from having to be a beauty, how does one win a beauty competition?

GAIL: I don't know whether you realise it or not, but you're asking for the story of my life!

PETER: I can take it!

GAIL: My father was a doctor, and at the age of sixty-four he died, not unexpectedly I am afraid, from cirrhosis of the liver. I was twenty-two at the time, and although I'd had very little secretarial experience I accepted a position as a confidential secretary to a gentleman by the name of Alderman Love. Alderman Love lived at Northsea, a small seaside resort about nine miles from Scarborough. He was a widower, but he had one son ... Tom. After I'd been at Northsea for about eighteen months, the local council decided to hold a sort of ... well, I suppose you'd call it ... a carnival week, and Alderman Love was put in full charge of the catering. He was naturally rather delighted about this because it afforded him ...

FADE IN of music. It is music which indicates a definite flashback.

The music FADES DOWN for the voice of ALDERMAN LOVE who has a rich Northern voice:

LOVE: Well, we seem to be getting a move on! Now, there's that there business with Wellings & Co.

GAIL: I've already written twice and they don't appear to take any notice, sir.

LOVE: Yes, well, we must 'ave patience, Miss Howard ... patience! That's what my Dad always used to say, and I've told our Tom the same ... If you don't 'ave patience you don't get anywhere. (*Irritated*) Not that

59

	our Tom will get very far, patience or no damn patience, the way he's carrying on!
GAIL:	(*Suddenly*) Oh, I've just remembered, sir, Councillor Stone rang up about ten-thirty … He wanted to know if you'd reached a decision.
LOVE:	Reached a decision …? What about?
GAIL:	I don't know, sir … that's all he said.
LOVE:	My word, he's a donkey that chap, an' no mistake!
GAIL:	(*Casually*) Would you sign this … and these two contract forms, please?
LOVE:	We're making a big mistake about this beauty competition … a big mistake!
GAIL:	Is it true you voted against it, Mr Love?
LOVE:	I should think it is true! An' a lot of the others would 'a' done likewise if they'd got 'alf-a-pennorth o' brains in their noodles! Beauty competition!!! What the 'ell do we want a beauty competition for?
GAIL:	(*Faintly surprised by LOVE's attitude*) Well … I think it's a grand idea. It's bound to attract a lot of people to Northsea, and surely that's the whole point of …
LOVE:	Yes, an' a rum lot too! We'll 'ave flappers bouncing in from Brid and Scarboro' an' from all over the blasted coast. (*Annoyed*) An' this stunt about Hollywood! Now that's a fine 'ow-do-you-do, if you like.
GAIL:	But surely you want the Carnival to be a success, and …
LOVE:	We want the class – the elite, as you might say. An' you don't get the elite mucking about in a beauty competition. Besides, there's some'at else – if one of our local lasses doesn't win it, there'll be a 'ell of a rumpus.

GAIL: But one of the local girls might win it.

LOVE: Don't be so daft! There isn't one of 'em worth looking at through the back end of a telescope – except that young wench our Tom keeps larkin' about with!

GAIL: Betty Reeves?

LOVE: Aye, Betty Reeves. (*Suddenly*) 'Ello, where's that estimate from Sandy Bros?

GAIL: It's on the desk.

LOVE: Aye, so it is! Can't see for looking!

The door opens and TOM LOVE enters. He is tall, extremely thin – and speaks with the accent, but not the authority, of his father.

TOM: Busy?

LOVE: (*With heavy sarcasm*) Busy? No! No, my lad! Come in! Come in. We've bags o' time.

The door closes.

TOM: I wanted a word with Miss Howard, father – if you don't mind.

LOVE: It's not for me to mind, my lad. (*To GAIL*) Well, I think I've got all I want ... for the time being at any rate. I'll be off! Don't be late, my dear.

GAIL: It's the Guildhall ...?

LOVE: Aye ... Guildhall.

The door opens and closes.

TOM: (*Awkwardly*) I hope I'm not butting in?

GAIL: Well, I've got rather a lot to do, just as the moment, Tom.

TOM: (*Worried*) Well – can we 'ave a talk later? I mean, it's so awkward like ... there's always either the old man 'anging around, or ...

GAIL: (*Quietly*) What is it, Tom?

TOM: (*Depressed*) Oh, I don't know ... I feel a bit fed up with things ...

GAIL: Is anything the matter?

TOM:	(*After a slight pause*) Yes. Yes, I'm worried ... I'm worried about this beauty competition ... It's proper getting on my nerves.
GAIL:	What do you mean?
TOM:	(*Depressed, irritated, and rather embarrassed*) Well, it's Betty ... She won't talk about anything else ... It's always this bloody competition.
GAIL:	(*Laughing*) Isn't that natural?
TOM:	In a way, I suppose ... yes ... but, I mean to say, she's so cocksure of 'erself ... so cocksure of winning it.
GAIL:	Well, she's certainly very pretty, Tom – I don't see why she shouldn't.
TOM:	That's right, cheer me up! Cheer me up!!!
GAIL:	(*Amused*) What are you so depressed about? If Betty won the competition ...
TOM:	If Betty won the competition, she'd go to Hollywood ... that's the first prize, isn't it? A free trip to Hollywood an' a six-month's contract with the H.G.T. studios. Now, I ask you ... if Betty Reeves clapped eyes on Hollywood would she ever want to come back to Northsea? ... By gum, it's not very likely, is it?
GAIL:	Oh, oh, I'm beginning to see daylight! So that's what's worrying you?
TOM:	(*With a sigh*) Aye, that's what's worrying me all right. Worryin' me good an' proper ... I can't even get any sleep through thinkin' about it.
GAIL:	(*Rather amused*) But – but what do you want me to do?
TOM:	Well ... (*Hesitatingly*) ... You see, it's like this: I'm pretty sure, in my own mind at any rate, that a local lass'll win the competition. She's almost bound to – I mean, if she didn't, well ...

GAIL: (*Imitating ALDERMAN LOVE*) There'd be a 'ell of a rumpus!

TOM: Not 'arf, there wouldn't. Well, that means Betty Reeves. Just as sure as my name's Tom Love – there isn't a skirt ... there isn't a lass in the district that can stand up to her, unless of course...

GAIL: Unless, of course ... what ...

TOM: Unless, of course, you decide to enter the competition, Miss Howard.

GAIL: (*Laughing*) Why ... Why I wouldn't stand an earthly!!!

TOM: Now, don't be daft! Why do you think you're working for the old man? There's nobody got a better eye for beauty than Alderman Love.

GAIL: But ... But in any case, I'm not a local girl and ...

TOM: Everyone looks upon you as being local – I mean ... You're living in the district ... You're well liked ... Popular with the lasses as well as the men folk – a point not to be sneezed at, either, by jingo!

GAIL: (*Laughing*) Yes, but ... Tom ... I – I couldn't enter the competition; I mean ... What would your father say?

TOM: Does it matter what Dad says? D'you intend to stay 'ere all your life ... In Northsea ...?

GAIL: Good heavens, no!

TOM: Then isn't this the chance you've been waiting for? I don't mind telling you if I was a young lass I wouldn't think twice about it. (*Puzzled*) What is it? What are you frightened of ...? Don't you want to go to Hollywood?

GAIL: Yes ... Yes, of course I do – but I don't exactly relish the idea of parading up and down the bathing pool in a sarong.

TOM: Parading up 'an' down be blowed! You've only got to walk round the pool once an' it's all over.

A slight pause.

GAIL: (*Thoughtfully*) Who's going to judge the competition?

TOM: A chap called Julius Markton ... or is it Markham? ... I don't know. He's one of the big pots in Hollywood, anyway ... at least Betty says so.

GAIL: Then this Hollywood offer ... is absolutely ... genuine ...? There's no catch in it?

TOM: Catch in it? O' course there isn't a catch in it! First prize ... two 'undred pounds, a free trip to Hollywood, an' a six-months' contract with the H.G.T. Studios. (*Anxiously*) Now what do you say, Miss Howard ... Are you goin' to have a shot at it?

GAIL: Well, it isn't to say I should win, Tom ... even if I did.

TOM: 'Course you'd win! An' if you didn't, then Betty certainly wouldn't ... an' that's all I'm worried about. (*Tensely anxious*) Now what do you say, Miss Howard ...? Come on, be a sport! What do you say?

GAIL: (*Quietly, rather amused*) I'll ... think about it, Tom. I'll think about it.

TOM: (*Delightedly*) Good!!! That's the girl!!!

GAIL laughs.

FADE IN music.

CROSSFADE to an excited background of enthusiastic spectators. The Northsea Brass Band are playing, with unbounded enthusiasm The March of the Gladiators.

There is a sudden burst of applause.

1st MAN: (*With enthusiasm*) That's the girl!!!

There is a second outburst from the crowd.

MARKHAM:	(*Quietly*) Yeah! … Yeah, that's the girl all right.
2nd MAN:	(*Pompously*) M'mm – She's not exactly a local girl, you know.
MARKHAM:	(*Bored*) Who cares? (*Raising his voice*) Would you kindly get the young lady over here?
1st MAN:	(*Fussy*) Certainly, Mr Markham! Certainly, Mr Markham! (*Shouting through a megaphone*) Number twenty-four … step this way, please. Number twenty-four!!!

The announcement is followed by applause.

The Brass Band moves forward.

There is another storm of applause.

MARKHAM:	Good afternoon, young lady!
GAIL:	Good afternoon.
1st MAN:	This is – er – Miss Howard … Miss Gail Howard … Mr Julius Markham …
MARKHAM:	So you want to go to Hollywood, Miss Howard?
GAIL:	(*Flippantly*) That seems to be more or less the idea, Mr Markham.
MARKHAM:	(*Amused*) O.K., young lady! You're on the way!!!
1st MAN:	(*Through the megaphone*) Winner of the Northsea Hollywood Beauty Competition … Miss Gail Howard!!!

FADE IN of applause.

FADE UP of the Brass Band.

Slow FADE DOWN … CROSSFADE to a private telephone exchange.

MAISIE:	(*Sing-song*) H.G.T. Studioes … Call for Mr Hartington … Hold the line, please … H.G.T. Studios … Call for Mr Markham … Hold the line, please … Sorry, Mr Foster's in Nebraska … Thank <u>you</u>, Mr Hartington … H.G.T. Studios …

	Call for Miss Charleston ... Hold the line, please ... Sorry, Miss Holt, Mr Foster's in Nebraska ... Hold the line, Mr Cheyne ... Miss Freeman wants you ... Go ahead, Miss Freeman ... H.G.T. Studios ... Call for Mr Hartington? ... Sorry ... Line engaged.
GAIL:	(*Meekly*) I – I beg your pardon, but could I see Mr Markham, please?
MAISIE:	Have you an appointment?
GAIL:	Well, I think he'll see me ... My name is Gail Howard, I won the Beauty Competition at Northsea ... last August.
MAISIE:	Who didn't? (*Pleasantly*) O.K., sister ... take it easy ... I'll do my best ... (*Suddenly*) Hello! You're lucky ... Here is Markham ...

A slight pause.

MARKHAM:	I'm expecting a call from Lord Mountrose – if he rings after twelve-thirty I shall be at The Blue Stetson.
MAISIE:	Yes, sir.

A tiny pause.

GAIL:	Mr Markham?
MARKHAM:	Yes?
GAIL:	(*Pleasantly*) I don't suppose you remember me, Mr Markham. I won the Beauty Competition at Northsea last ...
MARKHAM:	(*Offhand*) I'm afraid you'll have to excuse me – I've got a board meeting at eleven-fifteen. (*Turning*) Don't forget my message for Lord Mountrose, miss.
MAISIE:	No, sir.
GAIL:	Mr Markham, please!
MARKHAM:	(*Hesitating*) Perhaps you'd – er – like a word with my secretary ... Miss Rosenbloom?

GAIL: (*Finally exasperated*) I've had a word with Miss
                 Rosenbloom, Mr Markham. I've had a great
                 many words with Miss Rosenbloom ... In fact,
                 I've had lengthy and excessively monotonous
                 conversations with Miss Rosenbloom!

MARKHAM: Say, what seems to be the trouble?

GAIL: Six months ago, I won the Northsea Beauty
                 Competition, and I came to Hollywood. I came
                 to Hollywood to act, Mr Markham, to ...

MARKHAM: (*Interrupting GAIL*) My dear young lady, you
                 came to Hollywood because the H.G.T.
                 Corporation thought that you would be a great
                 deal more er ... accessible in Hollywood than
                 anywhere else. You know, what you beauty
                 contest girls have got to realise is that so far as
                 we are concerned you're ... just so many pots of
                 jam.

GAIL: Pots ... of ... jam!

MARKHAM: That's right! And it's easier for us to have you all
                 here ... on the shelf ... in Hollywood, than ...
                 say ... in Texas, or Nebraska, or New Orleans, or
                 Detroit, or New York, or ... Northsea! Don't
                 worry, one fine day, we'll take you off the shelf
                 all right ...

MARKHAM goes.

A tiny pause.

MAISIE: Yeah, they'll take you off the shelf, sister – when
                 Shirley Temple's drawing the old age pension
                 and Baby Sandy's a Grandpop.

GAIL: (*Almost to herself*) Well ... I must do something,
                 or I shall go mad! Besides, my contract expires
                 on Saturday ... and I'm nearly broke ...

MAISIE: Nearly broke? Well, listen ... there's a guy
                 called Joe Francino, he runs a filling station-

	cum-café about a hundred yards past The Gardens of Allah – if you don't mind wearing blue pants and a yellow beret he'll dish out thirty dollars a week.
GAIL:	But what for?
MAISIE:	You serve the customers with eats while Joe serves 'em with gas – just tell him Maisie sent you along, it'll be o.k.
GAIL:	Well ... you're very kind, Maisie.
MAISIE:	Think nothing of it! I know how you feel, kid! You see, I happen to be one of the pots of jam that guy Markham was talking about.
GAIL:	(*Softly, surprised*) You ...?
MAISIE:	Yeah ... Winner of the Bronxville Hollywood Beauty competition, Nineteen twenty-four!
GAIL:	(*Appalled*) Nineteen twenty-four! And ... they never took you off the shelf!
MAISIE:	Oh, yeah! They took me off the shelf all right, but I turned out to be a raspberry ... (*Suddenly, quickly*) H.G.T. Studios ... Call for Mr Shale? ... Hold the line, please ... H.G.T. Studios ... Call for Miss Charleston ... Hold the line, please ... (*FADE VOICE*) One moment, Miss Charleston ... Miss Ross-Cooper wants you ... H.G.T. Studios ... Sorry Mr Markham's not available ... (*FADE VOICE*)

FADE IN of music.

Quick FADE DOWN for the voice of JOE FRANCINO. He is an Italian-American – fat and friendly.

JOE:	You're doing swell, Rosie! No need to worry at all, Joe is a verra pleased with you!

GAIL:	(*Pleasantly, but rather tired*) Thank you, Mr Francino, but ... I do wish you wouldn't call me Rosie.
JOE:	But I like you ... I like you verra much, an' Rosie it is ... It is a nice name. Please! Please let Joe call you Rosie!
GAIL:	Yes, all right, Mr Francino.
JOE:	Oh, not Mr Francino! Why you always say ... Mr Francino? Joe ... It is plenty good enough for 'evra one else ... Why not call me Joe?
GAIL:	(*Rather wary*) Yes, all right, Mr Francino ... er ... Joe.
JOE:	Da's good ... You make Joe very happy ... It sound swell, eh? Joe an' Rosie ... Joe an' Rosie ... It sound verra good!

In the background a motor-horn is heard.

GAIL:	(*Laughing*) Well, we mustn't keep the customers waiting, Joe!

The horn is heard for the second time.

JOE:	Oh, ees always like that! Take a' no notice!
GAIL:	But he's been waiting five minutes – and he only ordered a waffle!
JOE:	All right ... all right ... you take the waffle, but tell him Joe is plenty annoyed.
GAIL:	(*Amused*) Yes ... O.K., Mr Francino!

Slow FADE IN of a car ticking over. The engine is switched off. JOCK REID, the owner of the car, is a middle-aged Scotsman.

JOCK:	What's the big idea?
GAIL:	Sorry to keep you waiting, Jock.
JOCK:	If I'd known this was going to happen, I'd have had my mail forwarded.
GAIL:	Here we are ... help yourself to syrup.
JOCK:	What do you call this ...? Is this wee piece of batter supposed to be a waffle!!!

GAIL: You'd better eat it while it's hot; do you want a paper to read?

JOCK: No … No, I've seen the papers, they're full of this Peter London business … I'm fed up to the blasted teeth with it!

There is a tiny pause.

GAIL: What do you mean … this Peter London business?

JOCK: The great Mr Hartington is looking for a guy called Peter London; he's supposed to have written a book called The Modern Pilgrim but nobody seems to have set eyes on him.

GAIL: Well, what does Hartington want him for?

JOCK: I suppose he's going to buy the film rights of the book – I don't know. I know one thing, they're kicking up a devil of a hullabaloo about it.

GAIL: But the name Peter London might be a pseudonym … perhaps even … the book was written by a woman.

JOCK: Oh, it isn't very likely! If it was a woman she'd be cashing in on the publicity, make no mistake about that.

GAIL: (*Quietly*) Cashing in on the publicity …? (*Thoughtfully*) Yes … Yes, I suppose she would …

There is a pause.

JOCK: What are you thinking about …?

GAIL: (*Suddenly*) M'mm? Oh … Oh, nothing! Would you like another waffle?

JOCK: Yes, but remember … I'm not here for the weekend!

GAIL: All right, Jock!

There is a FADE from the car to JOE. He is busy in the kitchen … When GAIL arrives, he is singing to himself.

JOE: Hello, Rosie! Another waffle …?

GAIL: Yes.

JOCK: (*Laughing*) I thought so … You know, da's man is verra funny, always he ask for one waffle when he mean two … maybe three … Sometime perhaps …

70

(*Suddenly*) What is it, Rosie? (*Alarmed*) You feel sick … maybe?

GAIL: (*Quietly*) Mr Francinco … When I came here, we agreed … didn't we? … that I could leave whenever I wanted to …

JOE: But, of course! (*Bewildered*) But – but you don't want to leave … not now?

GAIL: Yes … yes, I'm sorry, Mr Francino, but … I want to leave tomorrow …

There is a slight pause.

JOE: (*Bitterly*) It's this picture business! Always the same … this picture business … d'is stupid, cheap, dirty, goddam picture business!!!

GAIL: Mr Francino, please!

JOE: (*Hurt*) Don't a' Mr Francino me! I understan' … I understan' … You girls you mak' me sick … Always you think you're goin' to be the great star … But always you are the one a' hundred per cent flop! (*After a tiny pause*) Oh, Rosie! Rosie, my girl, don't be so stupid! You don't a' understand … Your name is mean nothing in this picture business … You are just a … A nonentity …

GAIL: (*Quietly, determined*) Yes, but I'm not going to remain a nonentity, Joe Francino … Oh, no! I'm going to be … Peter London …

JOE: (*Bewildered*) Peter London …?

FADE IN of music. It is the music which indicates a flashback.

We are returning from the flashback scenes. This music finishes. GAIL's voice FADES IN.

GAIL: … So now you know WHY I came to Hollywood … HOW I came to Hollywood, and WHY I decided to be … Peter London.

71

PETER: (*Amused*) And all because Tom Love wanted to marry Betty Reeves!

GAIL: Yes. But I'm afraid he didn't.

PETER: No?

GAIL: No. She married his father.

PETER laughs.

PETER: Would you like some more coffee …?

GAIL: Yes, I …

A gun shot is heard.

GAIL: (*Suddenly*) What is it?

PETER: (*Quietly*) Did you hear that …?

GAIL: What?

PETER: (*Hesitatingly*) I … thought … it sounded to me rather like … a revolver shot.

There is a pause. They are both listening.

GAIL: No – it must have been a car.

PETER: (*Thoughtfully*) Yes … Yes, it must have been … (*After a tiny pause*) Help yourself to milk …

GAIL: Thanks … (*Brightly*) Well, having told you in detail more or less the story of my life, I think a few personal reminiscences about yourself wouldn't be entirely out of place.

PETER: I was afraid of that! Well … what would you like to know?

GAIL: Are you … married?

PETER: No.

GAIL: Engaged?

PETER: No. (*An afterthought*) I was once in love with a school mistress …

GAIL: I see …

PETER: Not a … very good school mistress … of course.

GAIL: (*Amused*) Of course. Tell me, when did you write …

There is a knock on the door.

GAIL stops speaking.

PETER: (*Softly*) Listen!

There's another knock on the door.

GAIL: (*Tensely*) There's – there's someone at the door!

There is a third knock.

There is a pause.

A fourth knock is heard ... it is very faint ... and then another.

PETER: Yes ...

GAIL: (*Curiously*) Who is it? It can't be O'Hara ... Surely he wouldn't hesitate to ...

PETER: No! No! No! It can't be O'Hara ...

The knock is repeated.

From outside the door the voice of MARY BRAMPTON can be heard: "Mike! Mike! Mike! ...Open ... the ... door ..." She is obviously on the verge of a collapse ...

GAIL: (*Astonished*) It's ... It's a girl!

PETER: Yes!

The door is thrown open ... and MARY BRAMPTON falls into the room.

GAIL: She's – she's ... been shot ...! Look!

PETER: (*Grimly*) Yes ... help me to get her on to the settee ... Quickly!

GAIL: Who ... who is it?

PETER: It's that girl I told you about ... Mary Brampton ... She works for Markham.

GAIL: We'd better get a doctor, hadn't we ... I mean ...

PETER: Sh! Wait ... she's trying to say something ...

There is a pause.

MARY: (*Weakly*) I – I ... I know who killed ... Mr Hartington, it ... it ...

PETER: (*Anxiously*) Yes ... Yes ...

MARY: It was ... It ... was ... (*MARY's voice fails*)

GAIL: (*Alarmed and frightened*) Oh! She's ... She's dead ...

PETER: (*Softly*) Yes ...

FADE IN of music.

FADE DOWN of music.
FADE IN the voice of CAMPBELL MANSFIELD.

MANSFIELD: (*Bewildered*) But – but how perfectly extraordinary! I mean ... er ... what actually happened, did they decide to ...

SHALE: Well, after they realised that Mary Brampton had obviously been murdered, Peter decided that the ... (*Suddenly*) Holy smoke! Is ... Is that clock right?

MANSFIELD: M'mm? Oh, yes! Yes ... it's about right!

SHALE: Chee, I'd no idea it was that time! I'd – I'd better be making a move. I've got an appointment downtown at nine o'clock.

MANSFIELD: (*Excitedly, anxiously*) Yes ... Yes ... But ... But what happened? I mean to say ... you can't just leave the story like this ... I mean to say, it's ... er ... It's ...

SHALE: (*Chuckling*) Well, suppose we meet here next week ...

MANSFIELD: Yes ... Yes, rather! By all means!

SHALE: The same time?

MANSFIELD: Yes ... Yes, rather! By all means! (*With an amused, yet bewildered chuckle*) I mean to say ...

The cuckoo clock announces the time.

Cuckoo! Cuckoo! Cuckoo! Cuckoo! Cuckoo! Cuckoo! Cuckoo! Cuckoo! Cuckoo!

END OF EPISODE THREE

EPISODE FOUR

THE SECOND DEATH

| OPEN TO: | Cuckoo! Cuckoo! Cuckoo! Cuckoo! |
| | Cuckoo! Cuckoo! Cuckoo! Cuckoo! |

A second clock chimes the hour.

DALLAS SHALE arrives ... once again he is slightly out of breath through hurrying.

SHALE:	Hello ... Hello, there! Am I ... am I late?
MANSFIELD:	(*Laughing*) No later than usual! I've ordered a highball.
SHALE:	Oh, swell! (*Taking the drink*) Skoal!
MANSFIELD:	Cheerio!
SHALE:	(*After drinking*) Now let's see ... Where did I get to? ... With the story, I mean?
MANSFIELD:	Well, you told me that Oliver Hartington ... (*With a laugh*) ... in other words the Czar of Hollywood ... endeavoured to find a young novelist by the name of Peter London because he – that is Hartington – wanted to buy the film rights of Peter London's novel The Modern Pilgrim.
SHALE:	That's right. And one night, after Hartington had left for The Blue Stetson restaurant, a young girl appeared at the studio by the name of Gail Howard and ...
MANSFIELD:	And she said that ... she was Peter London ...
SHALE:	Correct! Anyway, we ... that is Julius Markham, the producer ... Louis Cheyne, the writer ... Margaret Freeman, the actress ... and Doris Charleston – Hartington's secretary – all dashed down to The Blue Stetson. When we arrived at the restaurant Hartington had already been murdered and Divisional-Inspector O'Hara was in charge of the proceedings. He was a rather quick tempered

little man but he very soon discovered that the waiter who served Hartington claimed to be none other than Peter London. At this moment I produced a cable for Mr Hartington ... which had just arrived ... and to our surprise it stated that Peter London would be ...

MANSFIELD: ...Arriving on the 2.30 plane from Indianapolis ... next Thursday.

SHALE: (*Laughing*) Yeah! At this point O'Hara lost his temper and sent Peter London – that is the waiter – and Gail Howard down to police headquarters. However they escaped, and eventually made their way to an apartment house on Lea Brea Avenue. While they were sitting in front of the fire having coffee they were interrupted by ...

FADE DALLAS SHALE's voice.

CROSS FADE to the knock on the door of the apartment house.

PETER: (*Softly*) Listen!

GAIL: (*Tensely*) There's – there's someone at the door!

PETER: Yes ...

GAIL: (*Anxiously*) Who is it? It can't be O'Hara ... Surely he wouldn't hesitate to ...

PETER: No! No! No! It can't be O'Hara ...

The knock is repeated.

From outside the door the voice of MARY BRAMPTON can be heard: "Mike! Mike! Mike! ...Open ... the ... door ..." She is obviously on the verge of a collapse ...

GAIL: (*Astonished*) It's ... It's a girl!

PETER: Yes!

The door is thrown open ... and MARY BRAMPTON falls into the room.

GAIL: She's – she's ... been shot ...! Look!

PETER: (*Grimly*) Yes ... help me to get her on to the settee ... Quickly!

GAIL: Who ... who is it

PETER: It's that girl I told you about ... Mary Brampton ... She works for Markham.

GAIL: We'd better get a doctor, hadn't we ... I mean ...

PETER: Sh! Wait ... she's trying to say something ...

There is a pause.

MARY: (*Weakly*) I – I ... I know who killed ... Mr Hartington, it ... it ...

PETER: (*Anxiously*) Yes ... Yes ...

MARY: It was ... It ... was ... (*MARY's voice fails*)

GAIL: (*Alarmed and frightened*) Oh! She's ... She's dead ...

PETER: (*Softly*) Yes ...

There is a slight pause.

GAIL: (*Quietly; desperately anxious*) What – what are we going to do?

PETER: There's only one thing we can do now ... we've got to give ourselves up and send for O'Hara.

GAIL: (*Alarmed*) O'Hara! But – but don't you see ... if he thinks that one of us killed Hartington then he's bound to think that ... we've ... we've done this ...

PETER: Yes. (*Suddenly*) Oh, my God, what fools we've been! What utter damn fools!

GAIL: What do you mean?

PETER: We ought never to have made a dash for it! I don't suppose for one moment that O'Hara thought that we'd murdered Hartington, so ...

GAIL: Then why did he send us down to police headquarters?

PETER: Because you said that you were Peter London ... because I said that I was Peter London ... and because of that confounded cable.

GAIL: (*Quietly*) Yes ... Yes, I suppose that's true.

PETER: I'm sorry. This business is entirely my fault, you ought never to have been ...

GAIL: Please! Please, don't be silly! (*With a little laugh*) We're in a jam ... and we've got to get out of it ... That's all there is to it!

PETER: (*Thoughtfully*) Yes ... Yes, but I don't quite see how, just at the moment.

GAIL: Do you think this girl knew what she was saying ... about Hartington?

PETER: Yes, she knew what she was saying all right ... poor kid.

GAIL: And you think that's why she was murdered?

PETER: Because she knew about Hartington? Yes ... Yes, I'm almost sure of it! (*Suddenly; having reached a decision*) You know, there's only one thing we can do about this business – we've got to send for O'Hara and make a clean breast of it. If we don't, things are going to pile up on us – and, before we know where we are, we're going to be in a devil of a fix!

GAIL: Yes, I don't doubt you're right, but O'Hara rather frightens me.

PETER: That's his technique, I'm afraid. (*Thoughtfully*) He was going back to the H.G.T. studios, wasn't he ... with the film people?

GAIL: Yes; but that's over an hour ago.

PETER: (*Lifting a telephone receiver: briskly*) We'll try there first ... anyway. (*On the phone*) Hello? ... Operator ... Could you get me the H.G.T. Studios, please? ... No, I'm afraid I don't know the number,

and ... Yes, it's urgent ... Very urgent ... M'm? ...
Oh, thanks! (*A pause*) Hello? (*Quickly*) H.G.T. ...?
Put me through to Mr Hartington's office ...
(*Impatiently*) Yes ... Yes ... I know all about that ...
I want to speak to Divisional-Inspector O'Hara ...
Yes, Divisional-Inspector O'Hara ... (*FADE
VOICE*)

FADE SCENE.

*FADE IN of a typewriter. It stops, and a piece of paper is
extracted.*

DORIS: Here we are!

O'HARA: Thanks.

DORIS: Is that all you want?

O'HARA: Yeah – that's all I want, for the time being.
            (*Thoughtfully*) M'm ... this list seems pretty
            impressive.

DORIS: Well, it should be! Don't forget it contains the
            names of more or less everyone that's been in
            continual contact with Mr Hartington during the
            past two years. You can check it up on our files, if
            you like.

O'HARA: (*Surprisingly pleasant*) No ... no ... no, I'll take
            your word for it, Miss Charleston ... for the time
            being. (*Perusing the list*) Hello! Who are these
            people ... the ones you've marked?

DORIS: They're the people you've already met.

O'HARA: Oh, yes! Yes, of course. (*Reading*) Dallas Shale,
            Scenario Department ... Oh, yes! Yes, I remember
            Mr Shale ... Louis Cheyne ... Louis Cheyne ...?
            Oh, he's the Englishman ... Yes ... Julius Markham
            ... Yes ... Margaret Freeman, the actress ... Yes ...
            Mary Brampton ... (*Puzzled*) Who's Mary
            Brampton? I don't seem to ... (*Suddenly*) Oh! Oh,

	the little secretary girl … I remember … Yes … Yes … Doris Charleston … Yes … M'm. Indeed … To be sure … Quite an impressive list, Miss Charleston… (*Pleasantly: matter of fact*) Oh, by the way, I've er – I've been meaning to ask you. How did these people get on with Hartington? I mean … were they … quite friendly towards him?
DORIS:	(*Faintly amused*) It was never a case of … how they reacted towards Mr Hartington; it was always a case of … how Mr Hartington reacted towards them.
O'HARA:	Yes. Yes, I suppose so. (*After a tiny pause*) Tell me, now that Hartington's dead … who … exactly … takes his place?
DORIS:	Oh, Mr Markham … I should say. At least, we've always had the impression that if anything happened to Hartington, Mr Markham would take over. He's a pretty big shareholder in the H.G.T. and M.O.M. combine.
O'HARA:	Oh, is he …? M'm … What about the Englishman … Cheyne?
DORIS:	Louis Cheyne …? Oh, he doesn't mean a thing! I suppose he's more or less what you'd call a … a well-paid hack writer. (*After a slight pause*) Although I suppose, in a way, this Hartington business is quite a lucky break so far as Louis is concerned.
O'HARA:	What makes you say that?
DORIS:	Well … you see, I happen to know that Mr Hartington didn't intend to renew his contract when it expires next month.
O'HARA:	Did Cheyne know that?
DORIS:	No. No … at least … I don't think so.
O'HARA:	M'm … (*Suddenly*) How did Miss Freeman get on with Hartington …?

DORIS: Oh … oh, very well … Mr Markham has a very
                high opinion of Miss Freeman's work.

O'HARA: Yes … yes, maybe … but I'm not talking about
                Markham, I'm talking about Mr Hartington.

DORIS: Yes, but you see … Mr Hartington always, more
                or less, accepted Mr Markham's – er – points of
                view … shall we say? … on matters relating to –
                er – artists.

O'HARA: I see. And did Miss Freeman … (*He is
                interrupted by the opening of the door. Quietly,
                but surprised*) Hello, Mr Markham! I … thought
                that you'd left … with the others?

MARKHAM: (*Slightly nervous: but gaining control of himself*)
                Yes ... yes, I did … only … I came back, I
                wanted to see you. (*Quietly*) What is it, Doris?
                What are you staring at? (*Suddenly: amused*) Oh!
                Oh, this sleeve! I bumped up against one of the
                railings they're painting on the Hamlet set … it
                is a nasty mess, isn't it! Looks as if I've been
                wallowing in blood or something!

O'HARA: What is it you – er – wanted to see me about?

MARKHAM: Oh, yes! You know that girl who came here …
                Gail Howard … the one that pretended to be
                Peter London?

DORIS: Yes.

O'HARA: I know the girl you mean …

MARKHAM: Well, you know it's damn funny – from the first
                moment I saw that girl I new darn well I'd seen
                her before somewhere. I've been trying to place
                her all night – and then suddenly, on the way
                home, it all came back to me. Her name really is
                Howard … Gail Howard … She won a beauty
                competition about … Oh, I should say about
                eighteen months ago …

83

O'HARA:	(*Interested*) Are you sure of this?
MARKHAM:	Absolutely! As a matter of fact she stopped me one night and … (*He stops. The telephone is ringing*)
DORIS:	(*Lifts the receiver; into the phone*) Hello? … Yes … Yes, he's here … Who is that speaking, please? (*Astonished*) What!!! (*Quickly*) Yes … Yes, hold the line!
O'HARA:	What is it?
MARKHAM:	What's the matter?
DORIS:	It's – it's Peter London … the waiter … the one that escaped …
O'HARA:	(*Staggered*) What!!!
DORIS:	He wants to talk to you …
O'HARA:	(*Excitedly*) Give me that phone!!! (*He takes the phone; on the phone*) Hello!!! … Yeah, this is O'Hara! … Now listen, wise guy! … What the hell is the big idea trying to … (*He hesitates*) What? (*A tiny pause*) Yeah … Yeah … I'm listening … (*A pause*) O.K. … What's it called? Sante …. What? … Sante Barbara … Lea Brea Avenue? … Yeah … Sure … O.K. … Yeah, right away … (*He replaces the receiver*)
MARKHAM:	(*Apprehensively*) What is it …?
DORIS:	Sante Barbara …? (*Suddenly*) Were you talking about Sante Barbara Apartment House … On Lea Brea Avenue?
O'HARA:	Yeah … why?
DORIS:	Well, oddly enough, that's where Mary Brampton lives, and … (*There is a pause*) … (*Slowly*) Nothing … Nothing's happened … to … Mary …?
O'HARA:	(*After a slight pause*) Yeah … she's been murdered …

MARKHAM: (*Softly: bewildered*) Murdered …?
DORIS: (*Weakly*) Oh, my God!
O'HARA: (*Suddenly*) Look out! She's going to faint!
FADE IN music. …

FADE DOWN music.
FADE IN DIVISIONAL-INSPECTOR O'HARA.
O'HARA: Yeah … yeah … go on … and then what
                  happened?
PETER: Well … then we decided that the only thing we
                  could do was … to send for you, and … make a
                  clean breast of it.
O'HARA: Do you expect me to believe that story?
PETER: It happens to be the truth.
GAIL: (*Suddenly very annoyed*) Now look here,
                  Inspector! It's – it's about time we had a
                  showdown! I don't know whether you are
                  labouring under the impression that we murdered
                  Mr Hartington or not, but I can …
O'HARA: Take it easy, young lady! Take it easy! (*He
                  chuckles*) You know this is kinda funny! I'd got
                  you two kids weighed up the moment I set eyes
                  on you.
GAIL: What do you mean?
O'HARA: I knew darn well that you'd got nothing to do
                  with the Hartington business.
PETER: Then why did you send us down to police
                  headquarters?
O'HARA: Because you got fresh! An' I don't like fresh
                  kids …
PETER: (*Quietly*) Inspector, we're in a spot … it's not a
                  bit of use our trying to kid ourselves that we're
                  not … because we are. Now if you want to make
                  things awkward for us …

85

O'HARA: I haven't the slightest wish to make things awkward for you! You play ball with me an' I'll play ball with you!

GAIL: (*Pleasantly*) Well, we've told you everything we know, we ... can't do more than that, Inspector.

O'HARA: Yeah ... well there's still one or two things I want to get straightened out. Now, for instance, if you're really Peter London ...

PETER: I am Peter London, Inspector.

O'HARA: Well ... if you're really Peter London why didn't you show up at the studios when there was all that newspaper ballyhoo?

PETER: For two reasons! Firstly: because I'm no longer interested in the picture business – I think it's a crazy, stupid racket! And secondly, because ... well ... because there wouldn't have been much point anyway.

O'HARA: How come?

PETER: Well, you see ... according to the newspapers Hartington wanted to buy the film rights of my novel The Modern Pilgrim.

O'HARA: Yeah ...

PETER: And I don't happen to own the film rights of The Modern Pilgrim. I parted with all the rights ... oh ... nine or ten years ago.

O'HARA: To a guy called Norman Roger Page?

PETER: (*Surprised*) Yes. Yes ... how did you know that?

O'HARA: That's o.k. ... (*Suddenly changing the subject*) This ... er ... this apartment doesn't belong to you, does it?

PETER: No. I've already explained that; it belongs to a friend of mine ... Mike Wendleford. He's on the camera staff at Metro. Just at the moment he's out on location ... I think in Mexico ... I'm not sure.

86

O'HARA:	Did this girl ... Mary Brampton ... know your friend?
PETER:	Why, yes! Yes, of course ...
GAIL:	That was almost the first thing we heard ... when she shouted ... "Open the door, Mike" ... wasn't it?
PETER:	Yes.
O'HARA:	Didn't you hear the shot?
PETER:	(*Thoughtfully*) Yes ... I rather think I heard it ... but I'm not sure. If I did, then ... it was quite a little while before she knocked on the door.
O'HARA:	(*Quietly*) Yes. (*After a tiny pause*) These apartments are fairly expensive, aren't they?
PETER:	I should imagine so ... yes.
O'HARA:	Mary Brampton's salary was just over a hundred and fifty dollars a month ... I checked up on it at the office.
PETER:	But I rather think she'd private means – at least, Mike always gave me that impression.
O'HARA:	M'm ... Did this friend of yours Mike ... er ...
PETER:	Wendleford.
O'HARA:	Mike Wendleford ... did he know that you were Peter London – the Peter London that Hartington was looking for?
PETER:	Yes, but he knew my opinion of the film people – and he also knew that I'd parted with the film rights of The Modern Pilgrim.
O'HARA:	I see. (*Thoughtfully*) You know, the thing that really makes me curious about this business ... is this cable ... the one that Dallas Shale gave me ... the one that was intended for Hartington ... Do you remember it? (*Reading*) "Have just received news from publishers ... Will arrive Hollywood 2.30 plane, Thursday ... Peter

London …" Now, if you really are Peter London … an' don't get excited now, because personally I believe that you are! … then … then who the heck sent this?

GAIL: Well, we can easily find out who sent it, can't we?

O'HARA: What do you mean?

PETER: What are you suggesting?

GAIL: I'm simply suggesting that we meet the 2.30 plane from Indianapolis … next Thursday …

FADE IN music.

Slow FADE DOWN music.
In the background can be heard general chatter and restaurant noises.

WAITRESS: Can I get you anything else?

O'HARA: Would you like some coffee?

GAIL: Peter …?

PETER: Yes … yes, I think so.

O'HARA: O.K. … coffee for two, miss. (*Suddenly*) Oh … Oh, an' by the way … do you happen to know where Mr Regan's office is …?

WAITRESS: Mr Regan?

O'HARA: Yeah … he's the Passenger Controller.

WAITRESS: Oh, yes … yes, I know the man you mean. You'll find his office through the main entrance hall … I think it's on the left.

O'HARA: O.K. … thanks. (*To PETER and GAIL*) I'll see you two downstairs, in about five minutes.

PETER: What time is it now?

O'HARA: It's nearly twenty past, but I believe the plane's late. Wait for me near the barrier … you know the spot I mean … near the ticket people.

PETER: Yes, all right …

O'HARA: See you both later!
FADE DOWN of restaurant noises.

*FADE UP of noises belonging to the Main entrance hall ...
outside, in the open, several aeroplane engines can be heard
ticking over.*
*There is a knock – then a door opens and closes. The background
noises have faded down.*

REGAN: (*Surprised*) Who are you?
O'HARA: Divisional-Inspector O'Hara ... Mr Regan?
REGAN: Yes?
O'HARA: I want a list of all the passengers that are arriving on
           the 2.30 plane from Indianapolis.
REGAN: Er – yes. Yes, certainly, Inspector ... Take a seat ...
           (*Turning the papers on his desk*) Now let me see ...
           2.30 from Indianapolis ... That's a ... Ah, here we
           are! ... M'm ... m'm ... er ... are you looking for
           anyone in particular?
O'HARA: Why do you ask?
REGAN: (*Faintly amused*) Well, it's ... it's a peculiar list, so
           far as I can see.
O'HARA: What do you mean ... peculiar?
REGAN: Well, all the passengers are girls ... young ladies,
           perhaps, I should say ... there isn't a man aboard ...
O'HARA: (*Bewildered*) Are ... are you sure?
REGAN: Absolutely ...
O'HARA: Are all the girls together; I mean ...
REGAN: Yes ... yes ... they call themselves The Manhattan
           Follies ... here's the list ... Miss Lea ... Miss
           Thompson ... Miss Forty ... Miss Harper ... Miss
           London ... Miss Crouch ... Miss ...
O'HARA: Did you say ... Miss London?
REGAN: Er – yes ... yes, that's right.

O'HARA: (*Springing into action*) O.K. Mr Regan! O.K.!!! An'
           many thanks.
REGAN: Think nothing of it …
The door opens.
FADE IN the noises belonging to the main entrance hall.
FADE UP of noises.
An aeroplane can be heard.
GAIL: Here's the Inspector …
O'HARA: (*Slightly out of breath*) Hello! Is … is that the plane
           …?
PETER: Yes. (*After a tiny pause*) You seem pretty excited,
           did you find out anything?
O'HARA: M'm – m'm … he's getting ready to land, isn't he?
GAIL: It rather looks like it …
There is a pause.
The aeroplane draws nearer, the noise of the engine increases.
*As the aeroplane lands the noise of the engine rises then
gradually diminishes until it finally stops.*

*FADE IN of a great many excited, and apparently highly
amused, young ladies who make their way to the barrier.*
O'HARA: (*Raising his voice*) Will all you young ladies kindly
           step over here, please!
1ˢᵗ GIRL: What is this?
2ⁿᵈ GIRL: Who is this guy?
3ʳᵈ GIRL: What's the trouble … tall, dark and handsome?
O'HARA: Which of you is … is Miss London?
1ˢᵗ GIRL: Is this a gag?
2ⁿᵈ GIRL: Listen brother, you've got a nice kind face but we're
           in no mood for fun and frolics …
O'HARA: My name is Divisional-Inspector O'Hara … and I
           want to talk to Miss London!
1ˢᵗ GIRL: So what?

2nd GIRL: Don't look at me, Clark Gable … I'm Rita Thompson …

O'HARA: (*Annoyed*) Which of you gals is Miss London …?

1st GIRL: We've never heard of the dame …

O'HARA: (*Exasperated*) Now listen! I'm in no mood for monkey business, if the gal doesn't step forward …

1st GIRL: (*Irritated*) How can she step forward, dope! We don't even know who she is!!!

O'HARA: I've – I've … a damn good mind to run you gals down to Police headquarters … the … the whole blasted bunch of you!!!

The girls laugh.

O'HARA: (*Furious*) What's your name!!!

2nd GIRL: Mickey Mouse.

O'HARA: Oh! Oh … so you're … you're goin' to be funny, eh?

1st GIRL: (*Aside*) He's quick you know …

2nd GIRL: (*Playing up*) Oh, you've got to give the guy credit!

O'HARA: (*Breathless with exasperation*) Now listen … Now listen … I'm … I'm … a very patient sort of guy, but …

1st GIRL: And handsome too.

There is general laughter.

O'HARA: (*Completely exhausted*) Oh … oh, my God!

MR REGAN suddenly arrives.

REGAN: (*Apologetically*) Say, Inspector, I'm so terribly sorry … my secretary got two of the names wrong on the Indiana passenger list. Apparently the list was phoned through and it was a bad line, and … Anyway, instead of Crouch it should be Grange …

1st GIRL: That's me brother … Tessa Grange …

REGAN: And instead of London it should be Logan …

2nd GIRL: Fifi to you, Inspector!

REGAN: I'm … I'm … awfully sorry, but … (*With a little laugh*) … accidents will happen … I guess.

O'HARA: (*Weakly*) Think nothing of it …

FADE IN music.

FADE DOWN music.

FADE IN the voice of CAMPBELL MANSFIELD.

MANSFIELD: (*Astonished*) Well, this story really takes the prize! You mean to say that no one turned up at the airport … that is … no one who claimed to be Peter London?

SHALE: (*Amused*) No one who claimed to be Peter London.

MANSFIELD: Then who on earth sent that cable …?

SHALE: (*Laughing*) D'you mind if I have another highball?

MANSFIELD: No. No, go ahead.

SHALE: The same again, Charlie! (*After a tiny pause*) Now what was I about to …? Oh! … the cable … Yeah … Yeah … the cable … Well, the cable which arrived for Hartington, and which said … "…Will arrive Hollywood 2.30 plane Thursday, Peter London …" was sent by a guy called Leo Bartlett.

MANSFIELD: Leo Bartlett? Who on earth is Leo Bartlett?

SHALE: Well, as a matter of fact, he used to be Margaret Freeman's husband.

MANSFIELD: Margaret Freeman's … husband?

SHALE: Yeah! And while O'Hara, Peter London and Gail Howard were at the airport, Margaret went down to the railway station … You see, she was meeting the 2.45 train from … Indianapolis.

FADE IN of music.

Quick CROSSFADE to the sound of a car.

The car draws to a standstill. The engine is switched off ... the car door slams.

FADE UP background noises of a very busy railway platform. The train draws into the station. A great many people emerge onto the platform.

A pause.
LEO BARTLETT meets MARGARET. He is a suave, extremely self-confident, Englishman.

LEO: My dear Margaret! This is quite delightful ... and how very nice to see you again! You're looking very sweet, my dear!

MARGARET: Leo ... can you leave your things here ... at the station ...? I want to talk to you before ... before you make any arrangements.

LEO: Why, yes ... of course! Have you the car?

MARGARET: Yes ... yes, it's on the drive.

LEO: Then suppose we meet at the car in ... say, about five minutes?

MARGARET: (*Quietly*) Yes ... all right, Leo. It's a blue Cadillac ... (*After a tiny pause*) Why are you smiling?

LEO: Was I smiling? Then it must have been because I rather expected you to have a blue Cadillac. (*Moving away*) Five minutes, Margaret!

FADE DOWN of the station noises.
The car door opens.

MARGARET: (*Surprised*) You haven't been long!

LEO: I never did have many virtues, did I? But punctuality was always one of them.

MARGARET: Leo ...

LEO: Yes, my dear?

MARGARET: I want you to go back to Indianapolis.

LEO:	(*After a tiny pause*) Is that why you asked me to leave my things at the station?
MARGARET:	Yes.
LEO:	You must forgive my apparent curiosity, Margaret – but did you send for me simply for the pleasure of a three minute conversation, or had you an ulterior motive which no longer exists?
MARGARET:	You got my letter?
LEO:	Ah, yes! Yes ... the letter! I was forgetting about the letter. Tell me: why did you want me to impersonate this writer fellow ... Peter London? Oh, I know that Hartington was searching for him; it was in all the newspapers from Timbuctoo to Tooting – but why particularly did you want me to impersonate him?
MARGARET:	Hartington intended – at least we all thought he intended to make a film of The Modern Pilgrim. I was scheduled to play the lead. Nothing could be started however until Hartington discovered Peter London. I – I got rather rattled. I knew that if things dragged on Hartington might change his mind, about me playing the lead, I mean ... and so I thought, it might be quite a good idea if ... if you ... impersonated ...
LEO:	If I impersonated Peter London? I see. Well, I'll say one thing for you, Margaret, success doesn't seem to have deprived you of any of your – er – persuasive powers.
MARGARET:	(*With a slight laugh*) Yes, well right now I'm trying to persuade you to go straight back to Indianapolis, Leo.

LEO:	But why, my sweet? Just because Hartington's dead it doesn't …
MARGARET:	I don't think you quite understand the position. The <u>real</u> Peter London is here … here in Hollywood.
LEO:	Is he, by jove? My word, now that is interesting. Then – er – what actually happened when they received my cable?
MARGARET:	It was taken straight to the police. They're watching the airport this very minute. That's why I cabled you about coming by train.
LEO:	Oh. Oh … I'm beginning to see daylight. Incidentally, I suppose our dear Julius takes Hartington's place?
MARGARET:	Yes.
LEO:	Ah! Then I can quite understand that there's no necessity for me to remain in Hollywood.
MARGARET:	What do you mean?
LEO:	Why, with dear Julius in charge, surely your worries are over? You're sitting pretty and I must confess that it rather suits you.
MARGARET:	Markham's always had a very high opinion of my work, you can't blame me for that, Leo!
LEO:	Blame you, Margaret? My dear, that would be the last thing I should do.

There is a slight pause.

MARGARET:	There's a train back to Indianapolis at 4.45, I hope that …
LEO:	I hope that you are not labouring under the impression that I'm going to catch it, because I can assure you that I haven't the slightest intention of doing so. Cigarette, my dear?
MARGARET:	Then you're going to stay … in Hollywood?
LEO:	Shall we say – for the time being?

MARGARET:	(*After a slight hesitation*) Leo, I don't want you in Hollywood, I don't even want you in California ... Go back to Indiana and I'll give you five thousand dollars.
LEO:	(*Ignoring MARGARET's remarks completely*) Cigarette?
MARGARET:	Did you hear what I said?
LEO:	Yes ... yes, I heard what you said all right.
MARGARET:	And your answer?
LEO:	My answer, dear Margaret, is what you expect ... No! I came to Hollywood quite prepared to do you a favour. To impersonate ... to play the part if you like ... of Peter London. Through circumstances which have since developed that becomes no longer necessary. But I haven't the slightest intention of returning to Indianapolis just because you ... choose to snap your fingers and offer me five thousand dollars.
MARGARET:	Then ... what do you intend to do?
LEO:	I've already told you. I intend to remain in Hollywood ... for the time being at any rate.

There is a pause.

MARGARET:	(*Quietly*) You seem very sure of yourself, Leo.
LEO:	I feel very sure of myself, Margaret.
MARGARET:	You've got something up your sleeve, haven't you?

There is a slight pause.
LEO is greatly amused.

MARGARET:	Why – why are you laughing?
LEO:	I am laughing because you offered me five thousand dollars to return to Indiana.
MARGARET:	Is five thousand dollars to be laughed at then?
LEO:	When you have information which is worth at least twenty-five thousand dollars ... yes!

96

MARGARET:	What – what do you mean?
LEO:	(*Pleasantly*) You see, Margaret ... I happen to know who killed Mr Hartington.

FADE IN music.

Slow FADE DOWN.
FADE IN the voice of DALLAS SHALE.

SHALE:	... So when Margaret realised that Leo was perfectly serious and was not merely endeavouring to create ... (*Suddenly*) Holy mackerel! Is ... is that clock right?
MANSFIELD:	I think so.
SHALE:	Time surely flies when you're telling a good tale, doesn't it?
MANSFIELD:	Oh no! You don't mean ...?
SHALE:	I'm afraid I do. I must fly!
MANSFIELD:	But – but, you can't leave it there!
SHALE:	Next week, my friend? Same place? Same time?
MANSFIELD:	(*Disappointed*) I suppose so ...

The cuckoo clock announces the time.

Cuckoo! Cuckoo! Cuckoo! Cuckoo! Cuckoo!
Cuckoo! Cuckoo! Cuckoo! Cuckoo!

END OF EPISODE FOUR

EPISODE FIVE

THE BLUE STETSON

OPEN TO: Cuckoo! Cuckoo! Cuckoo! Cuckoo!
                     Cuckoo! Cuckoo! Cuckoo! Cuckoo!

A second clock chimes the hour.

CAMPBELL MANSFIELD arrives ... he is rather out of breath.

MANSFIELD: I say ... I'm most awfully sorry ... I ... I never thought for ... for ...

SHALE: *(Amused)* That's o.k. ... Will you have a drink?

MANSFIELD: No! No! No! This is on me ... please! Two ... Two highballs, Charlie.

SHALE: Well, how are you liking Hollywood, Mr Mansfield?

MANSFIELD: Oh, I like it all right ... but it certainly takes a lot of getting used to.

SHALE: I'll say! Ah! Thanks, Charlie!

MANSFIELD: Thank you. Well ... cheerio!

SHALE: Skol! *(After a slight pause)* Now let's see, where did I get to? ... With the story, I mean.

MANSFIELD: Well, you told me that Oliver Hartington ... in other words the Czar of Hollywood ... endeavoured to find a young novelist by the name of Peter London – and that one night Hartington was found mysteriously murdered in The Blue Stetson restaurant.

SHALE: Correct! Well, when we ... that is Julius Markham, the producer ... Louis Cheyne, the writer ... Margaret Freeman, the actress ... and Doris Charleston – Hartington's secretary – arrived at the restaurant we discovered that Divisional-Inspector O'Hara was in charge of the proceedings. O'Hara very soon discovered that the waiter who served Hartington claimed to be none other than Peter London. At this moment I produced a cablegram for Mr

	Hartington … which had just arrived … and to our surprise it stated that Peter London would be …
MANSFIELD:	… arriving on the 2.30 plane from Indianapolis … next Thursday.
SHALE:	Correct! But the following Thursday, when Divisional-Inspector O'Hara, Peter London – that is the waiter – and a girl called Gail Howard arrived at the airport, no one answering to the name of Peter London arrived on the 2.30 plane from Indianapolis. Meanwhile, Leo Bartlett – Margaret Freeman's ex-husband – arrives at the railway station. Leo is the person responsible for the mysterious cablegram and at Margaret's request …
MANSFIELD:	… He has come to Hollywood to impersonate Peter London!
SHALE:	Exactly! Margaret however, because of recent events, has changed her mind about this, and she now begs Leo to return to Indianapolis. But Leo is a strange, and rather self-confident person. He feels that now he has returned to California … *FADE VOICE*

CROSSFADE to the voice of MARGARET FREEMAN.
MARGARET and LEO are in the car outside of the station.

MARGARET:	(*Quietly*) You seem very sure of yourself, Leo.
LEO:	I feel very sure of myself, Margaret.
MARGARET:	You've got something up your sleeve, haven't you?

There is a slight pause.
LEO is greatly amused.

| MARGARET: | Why – why are you laughing? |

LEO:	I am laughing because you offered me five thousand dollars to return to Indiana.
MARGARET:	Is five thousand dollars to be laughed at then?
LEO:	When you have information which is worth at least twenty-five thousand dollars ... yes!
MARGARET:	What – what do you mean?
LEO:	(*Pleasantly*) You see, Margaret ... I happen to know who killed Mr Hartington.

There is a slight pause.

MARGARET:	You ... happen to know who ... killed ... Mr Hartington?
LEO:	Yes.
MARGARET:	Are you serious?
LEO:	Perfectly serious.
MARGARET:	(*After a slight hesitation commences to laugh*) You are an extraordinary person, Leo!
LEO:	Am I, Margaret?
MARGARET:	(*Still apparently amused*) How – how could you possibly know who murdered Hartington? Why ... (*Somewhat apprehensively*) ... Why ... When Hartington was murdered you were in ... Indianapolis.
LEO:	Yes, but even in Indianapolis you can put two and two together.
MARGARET:	(*Laughing*) I suppose you read all about the murder in the newspapers and immediately concocted a simply marvellous theory!
LEO:	(*Completely matter of fact*) You know, Margaret, I always had the impression that you were an extremely bad actress and now I'm quite convinced of it. For the last thirty seconds you've been trying to impress upon me the fact that you simply don't believe I know who murdered Hartington, and that even if I did it

would be a matter of supreme indifference to you. Actually, you've succeeded in convincing me that you firmly believe that I do know who murdered Hartington and that you're ... er ... hellishly worried about it.

MARGARET: (*After a pause; annoyed*) You haven't altered in the slightest, Leo! You're just as stupid, just as conceited, just as self-centred as ... ever you were!

LEO: Thank you, my dear. (*Softly*) And you're just as sweet ... just as lovely as ever ... (*An afterthought*) ... but a shade stouter, Margaret ... of course.

MARGARET: (*Exasperated*) Every time we meet I ask myself over and over again why ... why ... in heaven's name! ... did I ever marry you?

LEO: Well, I trust you give yourself a satisfactory answer, because you certainly couldn't be asked a simpler question. You married me because you are, and because you always will be, at heart a snob. My father was the Duke of Rainford, a member of what, for the want of a better term we choose to call the landed gentry. Although just exactly what he was landed with Margaret has always been something of a mystery. On the other side of the fence ... your father was a draper. He lived in a small, and I'm told an extremely draughty little shop on the outskirts of Detroit. But whereas your father was undoubtedly an extremely good draper, my father was without question an extremely bad duke.

MARGARET: (*Grimly*) Leo, I am going to repeat the offer I
              made to you a few minutes ago. I am going to
              offer you five …
LEO: Don't waste your time, my dear. Will you
              excuse me? I want to get my things from the
              station. (*Suddenly*) Oh! Oh, and before I forget
              … I want you to have dinner with me tonight,
              Margaret, at The Blue Stetson.
MARGARET: I'm sorry, I'm dining with Julius.
LEO: I shall be staying at The Garden of Allah, so
              supposing you pick me up at about … oh, about
              nine-thirty.
MARGARET: I've told you, Leo, I'm dining with Julius
              Markham!
LEO: (*Pleasantly*) Nine-thirty, Margaret … at The
              Garden of Allah …

FADE Scene.

FADE UP of CAMPBELL MANSFIELD's voice.

MANSFIELD: (*Laughing*) Well, he certainly is a cool
              customer! Although, what I actually … Oh!
              Have another highball?
SHALE: Well – er – thanks … I don't mind if I do …
MANSFIELD: Another highball for Mr Shale! Now what was
              I saying? Oh … Oh, I remember … What I
              should like to know is … what happened at the
              airport when no one turned up – that is … no
              one pretending to be Peter London? (*Laughing*)
              O'Hara must have been livid!
SHALE: At first, yes … but I believe he very quickly
              calmed down. And then apparently the three of
              them … O'Hara … Peter London … and Gail
              Howard went back in the restaurant. Over
              coffee they discussed once again the …

FADE Scene.

FADE UP of O'HARA's voice.

O'HARA: (*To the WAITRESS*) Yeah … yeah, coffee for three, miss! (*Thoughtfully*) You know, that cable from Indianapolis might have been phoney, but it was no hoax – I'm pretty sure about that. Someone intended to come to Hollywood an' impersonate Peter London – and that someone changed his plans … now why?

GAIL: Well, the answer to that is pretty simple, Inspector, isn't it?

O'HARA: What do you mean?

GAIL: The person in question changed his plans for the very good reason that he discovered that Peter London – the real Peter London was here in Hollywood.

O'HARA: M'm … maybe … maybe …

PETER: You know, Inspector, I've got a feeling at the back of my mind that you don't really think I'm Peter London even now.

O'HARA: Oh, yeah … yeah, I believe you all right – if I didn't you wouldn't be here, sonny, don't make any mistake about that. But there's still one or two points I'm kinda hazy about.

PETER: Such as what?

O'HARA: Well, what makes the author of a best seller like The Modern Pilgrim work as an ordinary waiter in a restaurant? An' don't hand out that story about looking for local colour or I'll break down an' weep!

PETER: I thought I'd explained that to you, Inspector! In the first place The Modern Pilgrim is not, and never will be, a best seller. Hartington boosted it

106

because he liked it and wanted to buy the film rights. But I'd already sold the film rights, all the rights in fact ... for the sum of fifty pounds. (*After a tiny pause*) In any case, I thought you knew that? (*Puzzled*) You must have known it, because ... you mentioned the name of the agent I sold the rights to ... Norman Roger Page.

GAIL: Yes ... yes, of course you did!

PETER: (*Quietly*) How did you find out about ... Page?

O'HARA: I'll explain that later. But first of all ... tell me ... did you ever meet him?

PETER: Page? No, I never met him. He simply wrote me a letter, and made me an offer ... and I signed an agreement ... that's all there was to it.

GAIL: This was before the Hartington business?

PETER: Good heavens, yes! Let me see, it would be about six months after the book was published, and that ... Oh, about 1932, I should say.

O'HARA: (*Quietly*) Yes, August ... 1932 ... I found the agreement in Hartington's desk.

PETER: (*Staggered*) In Hartington's desk!

GAIL: Are – are you joking?

O'HARA: No. No, I'm quite serious.

GAIL: But – but if you found the agreement in Hartington's desk then ... then he had the film rights of The Modern Pilgrim!

O'HARA: Yes.

GAIL: But if Hartington had already got the film rights then what on earth was all the newspaper ballyhoo about?

PETER: Yes ... What else did he want?

O'HARA: He wanted you.

PETER: Me! (*With a laugh*) I'm afraid I don't understand.

O'HARA: Hartington, judging from all accounts, was a rather impetuous sort of guy – and apparently when he read your book The Modern Pilgrim he made up his mind that he was going to bring the man who wrote it to Hollywood and put him in complete charge of the H.G.T. scenario departments. Naturally, Hartington knew that the suggestion would meet with a certain amount of opposition so he let everyone think that he was merely interested in the film rights of the novel and simply wanted to meet Peter London in order to discuss the – er – usual details.

PETER: (*Amazed*) Are – are you sure of this?

O'HARA: Oh, absolutely!

GAIL: But that still doesn't explain about the agreement … about it being found in Hartington's desk, I mean.

O'HARA: No.

PETER: How did you find out about all this, Inspector?

O'HARA: About the fact that Hartington wanted you, and not the rights of the novel? Doris Charleston told me.

GAIL: Did any of the other film people know the true position?

O'HARA: I don't think so. In fact I'm sure they didn't. They all seemed pretty well bowled over when they heard about it from Doris. (*Suddenly*) Why do you ask?

GAIL: (*Thoughtfully*) I'm just thinking … supposing someone knew that this agent Norman Roger Page had the film rights of The Modern Pilgrim, and the moment Hartington started his publicity campaign he bought the agreement from the agent and then tried to sell it at a profit to Mr Hartington … only to discover that Hartington didn't want the agreement at all, but simply wanted the services of the author. It would be rather a nasty position for the person concerned, wouldn't it? Especially if he'd already paid Norman Roger Page a fairly big sum.

O'HARA: Yeah … yeah. That's quite a theory.

GAIL: And that isn't everything either. Supposing Hartington didn't happen to like this particular person – the man who bought the agreement I mean. He'd get quite a kick out of it, wouldn't he?

O'HARA: Yeah … yeah, you can just imagine Hartington offering the guy chicken feed for something he'd probably paid about ten thousand dollars for.

PETER: That certainly provides a motive, so far as Hartington's concerned … but how does Mary Brampton fit into this?

O'HARA: Mary Brampton was Markham's secretary, but she worked for Hartington for about a fortnight when Doris Charleston was ill.

GAIL: And during that fortnight the poor girl must have found out something … something of importance.

PETER: Yes. You never know, she might possibly have overheard the scene between Hartington and the person who had the agreement.

O'HARA: Yeah! Yeah, that's very likely!

GAIL: Inspector, have you made any attempt to try and trace the agent … Norman Roger Page?

O'HARA: Sure, but it seems pretty hopeless. Apparently he left New York in 1933 and … well, that's all we can find out about the guy.

GAIL: You don't think he's here in Hollywood?

O'HARA: (*Surprised*) Here … in Hollywood?

GAIL:	Yes. You know, we might not be quite right with our theory. Supposing Page went to Hartington … himself … and tried to sell the agreement.
O'HARA:	M'm … I suppose that's possible …
PETER:	(*Quietly*) Yes, and supposing his real name isn't Norman Roger Page, but … Julius Markham.
O'HARA:	(*Surprised*) Julius Markham!
PETER:	Or Louis Cheyne, or Doris Charleston, or …
O'HARA:	My God, it might be one of the film people at that!
GAIL:	Yes …
PETER:	(*Thoughtfully*) It's a pity I'm not still at The Blue Stetson. A waiter often hears things, and sees things too, that the average person overlooks.
O'HARA:	Yeah … yeah, I reckon that's true! (*After a tiny pause*) Who's the head man at The Blue Stetson?
PETER:	A Mr Sylvestor.
O'HARA:	Well, Mr Sylvestor doesn't know it yet, brother – but you're back on the payroll.

FADE IN music.

Slow FADE DOWN music.

FADE IN of cafeteria noises. Somewhere in the background, a piano can be heard.

| SAM: | (*Faintly exasperated*) Move along, please! Now move along, please! Get your tray at the other end, sir … Yeah … yeah, pay at the desk … |

A female voice is heard protesting about the service.

| SAM: | Take it easy, lady! Take it easy! Say listen, this is a cafeteria – it's up to you how good the service is! Get your tray at the other end, sir … Keep moving, please! |

FADE away from SAM's voice.

FADE IN PETER and GAIL. They appear to be greatly enjoying themselves.

GAIL: (*Laughing*) I shall never eat all this ... it's – it's ridiculous!

PETER: Nonsense! (*Suddenly*) Ah! Hot chocolate sauce!!!

GAIL: (*With a groan*) Oh, not hot chocolate sauce, please!

PETER: (*Laughing*) O.K. ...

GAIL: Where shall we sit?

PETER: There's a table ... over in the corner!

GAIL: Oh, yes.

FADE DOWN of cafeteria noises ... the piano stops.

PETER: Well ... this looks to me to be pretty good!

GAIL: Hungry?

PETER: Yes. Yes, I am rather.

GAIL: What time are you due at The Blue Stetson?

PETER: About six-thirty ... sugar?

GAIL: Thanks. (*After a tiny pause*) Are you pleased that you're going back to the restaurant?

PETER: No, I'm not – not really. I suppose I was a bit of a fool to mention the idea to O'Hara. Still, if it helps to clear this Hartington business up I shan't mind.

GAIL: Do you think it will help to clear it up?

PETER: (*Enjoying his meal*) What d'you mean?

GAIL: Well ... do you think that you'll find out something which might ... er ... show who murdered Mr Hartington?

PETER: I don't know about that: that's rather a tall order, isn't it?

GAIL: (*Thoughtfully*) Hartington was poisoned, wasn't he?

PETER: Yes. With cyanide, but you know the extraordinary part about it is that they didn't find any cyanide in the food.

GAIL: Perhaps he'd taken the poison before he came to The Blue Stetson.

PETER: No. I'm afraid that's not possible. You see, after the autopsy, the doctor definitely stated that Hartington had taken the poison about fifteen minutes before he died.

He was at The Blue Stetson for ... oh ... almost two hours.

GAIL: M'm. (*After a pause*) You don't think Hartington committed suicide?

PETER: Committed suicide? (*Thoughtfully*) I don't know ... (*Suddenly*) Still, O'Hara certainly doesn't think so.

GAIL: Yes – but he's got no actual proof that he didn't commit suicide. In fact, he doesn't really know how Hartington died.

PETER: (*Faintly amused*) What do you mean ...? Of course he does! Hartington was poisoned with cyanide.

GAIL: Yes, but how did he take the cyanide, that's the point?

PETER: (*Quietly*) Well, he certainly didn't get it served up to him, I'm sure about that.

GAIL: What did Hartington eat, can you remember?

PETER: (*Suddenly: amused*) I say, what is all this? You're – you're a darn sight worse than O'Hara.

GAIL: No. No, really – I'm quite serious.

PETER: Well, he had some tomato soup ... a grilled sole ... black coffee ... and a dyspepsia tablet.

GAIL: A dyspepsia tablet?

PETER: Yes, believe it or not the great Mr Hartington suffered from dyspepsia – and how he suffered! Oh, and you needn't think the dyspepsia tablet had anything to with it, because he left half a bottle behind and they were perfectly all right – that was the first thing the doctor went for. (*Suddenly*) Look here, let's stop talking about Hartington!

GAIL: Well, what would you like to talk about?

PETER: You.

GAIL: Me?

PETER: Yes. I suppose you know that you're a frightfully attractive person.

GAIL: Frightfully attractive. Apple pie.

112

PETER: I beg your pardon?

GAIL: The … apple pie.

PETER: Oh, I'm so sorry … (*He passes GAIL the apple pie*)

A tiny pause.

GAIL: M'm … this is delicious.

PETER: Gail, tell me … what do you want to do?

GAIL: What do I want to do? What – what do you mean exactly?

PETER: I mean … so far as Hollywood is concerned. Do you intend to go on the films or …

GAIL: I say, just a minute, don't you think it's my turn to ask a few questions? Don't forget I've already told you the story of my life!

PETER: (*Laughing*) Yes. Yes, perhaps you're right.

GAIL: Supposing this Hartington business is settled, then … what do you intend to do?

PETER: (*Vaguely*) Oh, I don't know … sort of knock around, I guess. (*Quickly*) Have some more apple pie …

GAIL: Look here young man, don't be so evasive!

PETER: Well, the fact of the matter is … I don't really know what I want to do. I started off by writing a novel, and …

GAIL: The Modern Pilgrim?

PETER: Oh, no … that came later – much later. This was a novel of ancient Rome … it – er – it was written from the point of view of a Roman Gladiator …

GAIL: I see.

PETER: (*Almost an afterthought*) The spelling was awfully good.

Gail laughs.

GAIL: Would you like some more coffee?

PETER: M'm? Oh, thanks! (*After a tiny pause*) Would you mind terribly if I asked you a rather personal question?

GAIL: I thought I was asking the questions?

PETER:	Oh … Oh, I'm sorry.
GAIL:	No, please … What were you going to say?
PETER:	I was going to say … Gail … Have you ever been in love?
GAIL:	(*After a slight pause*) Once … it was a long time ago.

The piano starts again. It is playing a sentimental waltz.

PETER:	What happened?
GAIL:	Oh … so many things.
PETER:	(*Anxiously*) You're not in love any longer … are you …? (*Quickly*) With … with the same person, I mean.
GAIL:	(*Faintly amused*) No … no, I'm not in love any longer … with the same person …
PETER:	(*Absolutely delighted: yet confused*) Oh … oh, well … that's er … that's absolutely … er … absolutely … er … well … we … (*Quickly*) Have – have some more apple pie!

GAIL laughs.
FADE In music.

FADE DOWN music.
CROSSFADE to the sound of a motor car. The car eventually draws to a standstill.
The car door opens.

MARGARET:	Wait here, Spencer, we shall be going on to The Blue Stetson.
SPENCER:	Yes, madam.

A pause.
MARGARET enters the big apartment house.

MAN:	Good evening, Miss Freeman.
MARGARET:	Good evening, Draper. Mr Bartlett's expecting me.

MAN: Yes, Miss Freeman ... Apartment 17 ... fourth
                 floor ...
MARGARET: Thank you.
A pause.
FADE IN of the lift which ascends and then stops.

FADE from the lift. A buzzer can he heard.
A door opens.
LEO: (*Pleasantly*) Ah, hello, Margaret! I'm nearly
                 ready ... Come inside, my dear.
The door closes.
MARGARET: Aren't you surprised to see me, Leo?
LEO: Surprised? Why, no! We said nine-thirty.
MARGARET: (*Pleasantly*) You said nine-thirty ...
LEO: (*With a little laugh*) The same thing, Margaret
                 ... Now ... what can I offer you? A Bronx ...?
                 A Manhattan ...? A gin and ...
MARGARET: I think I'd rather like ... a sherry ...
LEO: Certainly. (*He mixes the drinks*)
MARGARET: (*Studying the apartment*) M'm ... You've done
                 yourself rather well, haven't you, Leo?
LEO: Oh ... it'll do ... it'll do, for the time being.
                 Your ... sherry ...
MARGARET: Oh, thank you.
LEO: (*Raising his glass*) Well, Margaret ... your
                 health, my dear ... and long may your classic
                 features flicker across the silver screen ...
MARGARET: To your return to Indiana ...
They drink.
LEO: Well, it must be four years, Margaret, since we
                 last had dinner together.
MARGARET: Yes, at least four years.
LEO: (*After a tiny pause*) You look rather pleased
                 with yourself tonight ...

MARGARET: Yes, I feel rather pleased with myself, Leo.

A slight pause.

LEO: They keep you fairly busy, don't they, Margaret?

MARGARET: Oh, yes. I've made three films in the last eighteen months.

LEO: M'm.

MARGARET: Did you see my last picture?

LEO: No, I'm afraid I didn't. I ... er ... I saw the trailer. (*Politely*) Another sherry, Margaret?

MARGARET: Thank you.

LEO: (*Mixing more drinks*) And what did our dear Julius say when you – er – called off your date?

MARGARET: Oh, but I didn't call it off ...

LEO: No?

MARGARET: (*Slightly amused*) No.

LEO: Does that mean we're to have the pleasure of Markham's company at ...

MARGARET: Julius telephoned me about an hour ago – he's dining with Carl Van Schulberg.

LEO: Schulberg ... the banker ...?

MARGARET: Yes, apparently he's just arrived from New York. Schulberg finances H.G.T. ... you know.

LEO: Does he? I didn't know that. My word, dear Julius is stepping out, and no mistake ... your sherry.

MARGARET: Thank you. (*After a slight pause*) Leo ...

LEO: Yes?

MARGARET: (*Really pleased with herself*) Do you know what Markham told me?

LEO: No.

MARGARET: H.G.T. are not going to make The Modern Pilgrim after all, they've bought the new Horace Wyndham Harringford story ...

LEO:	The Sky Is Always Dark? That must have cost them a packet!
MARGARET:	Nearly a hundred thousand.
LEO:	Good God! Who's going to play the part of Charlotte?
MARGARET:	Can't you guess?
LEO:	Hepburn? (*After a tiny pause: astonished*) Margaret ... Margaret ... you don't mean to say that ... that ... you're going to play the part of ... of Charlotte Early ...?
MARGARET:	Well, an' why not ... for Pete's sake?
LEO:	But – but it's a story about the American civil war ... it ... it takes place in Alabama ... Charlotte's supposed to be a young girl ... about ... oh! ... about eighteen ...
MARGARET:	(*Faintly exasperated*) I know! I know! I read The Saturday Evening Post ...
LEO:	She's a Southerner, Margaret ... a girl from Georgia ... a young innocent girl that has hardly set ...
MARGARET:	For cryin' out loud! Can't I be a Southerner ...?
LEO:	(*Quietly*) Does Markham think that you can ... play ... Charlotte Early ...?
MARGARET:	Of course he thinks that I can play Charlotte Early!
LEO:	Well, that's all you've got to worry about, Margaret. (*Raising his glass*) Your health, my dear ... and to what, I am sure, will be a most ... outstanding ... performance.
MARGARET:	(*In a broad Southern accent*) Well, now ... that's powerful nice of you, honey ... powerful nice ...

LEO groans. FADE IN music.
Slow FADE DOWN music

117

FADE IN of restaurant noises.

SYLVESTOR:	(*Pleasantly*) Good evening, Mr Horton …
EDWARD E. HORTON:	Hello, Sylvestor, how are you …? My … oh, my … looking fine, I must say … (*To his partner*) Careful, my dear … careful … (*He bumps into someone*) … Oh, my! Really, I … I beg your pardon … (*FADE away*)
SYLVESTOR:	Good evening, Mr Stewart …
JAMES STEWART:	You got my phone message all right …?
SYLVESTOR:	Yes, sir … the table is waiting for you.
JAMES STEWART:	Oh, swell!

A pause.

MARGARET and LEO arrive.

MARGARET:	Did you reserve a table?
LEO:	I did.
SYLVESTOR:	Good evening, Miss Freeman! Good evening, sir!
LEO:	Good evening … I reserved a table for ten-fifteen … Bartlett's the name …
SYLVESTOR:	Yes, sir.
MARGARET:	(*Softly: surprised*) Why, Sylvestor … you've got that waiter back … the one that said he … was … Peter London.
SYLVESTOR:	Yes, madam. (*In a whisper*) Confidentially, we had no alternative …
MARGARET:	Oh, I see.
LEO:	Which waiter is that?

118

MARGARET:	Over in the far corner.
LEO:	M'm – not a bad looking young fellow.
SYLVESTOR:	This way ... madam ... If you please, sir. (*He leads MARGARET and LEO to their table*)

A pause.

MARGARET:	(*Faintly annoyed*) Sylvestor ... is this the only table you've got?
SYLVESTOR:	I'm afraid it is, Miss Freeman, we're ... we're very full this evening.
MARGARET:	Yes, all right ...
SYLVESTOR:	Thank you, madam.

SYLVESTOR departs.

LEO:	What's the matter with you, Margaret? This is a perfect table ...
MARGARET:	It happens to be the table that Hartington always ... occupied ...
LEO:	Oh! (*Amused*) Well, you're not superstitious, my dear, surely ... not at your time of life.
PETER:	(*Passing the table*) I'll be with you in just one moment, sir.
LEO:	Yes, all right, waiter. (*Casually*) Cigarette, Margaret?
MARGARET:	(*Glancing round the room*) No ... no thank you.
LEO:	(*Laughing*) They're not my usual poisonous weeds from Mexico.
MARGARET:	No thank you, Leo. (*Suddenly*) Ah, there's Julius!
LEO:	And the gentleman with the Wall Street personality I take to be Carl Van Schulberg?
MARGARET:	Yes. (*Turning towards LEO; pleasantly*) Well ... what did you do with yourself this afternoon, Leo?

119

LEO:	That is a charming smile, Margaret, I feel sure it's more for Markham's benefit than mine. What did you say? What did I do this afternoon? Oh, I ... er ... bumped into one or two old friends.
MARGARET:	Such as ...?
LEO:	The usual film crowd ... Dallas Shale ... Louis Cheyne ... Mike Ronson ... Brett McNeal ...
MARGARET:	They would be surprised to see you!
LEO:	(*Amused*) Yes ... yes, they were ...
MARGARET:	Well, they say you can't keep a bad penny out of circulation, don't they, Leo? (*After a tiny pause*) Hello ... here's Julius!

A slight pause.

MARKHAM:	Hello, Margaret ... I'm sorry about tonight but you quite understand?
MARGARET:	(*With charm*) Of course, Julius!
MARKHAM:	One or two things have got to be straightened out, so I thought it better if Van came over for a day or two ... Oh, by the way, before I forget ... I want to see you tomorrow morning in my office ... about eleven-thirty ... (*Pleased with himself*) You ... know what it's about?
MARGARET:	Yes, I think so, Julius ...
MARKHAM:	We've paid a hundred thousand dollars for this story, Margaret, and ... (*After a slight pause*) What's the matter with your friend?
MARGARET:	Oh, I'm sorry, my dear. (*Turning towards LEO*) Leo, I want you to meet Julius Markham our new ... Leo! ...

A tiny pause.

MARGARET:	Leo! Don't be silly ... wake up ...
MARKHAM:	(*Laughing*) What's he trying to do ... impersonate Hartington? Is this some kind of

an audition for … (*He stops speaking, and the moment he does so LEO falls forward across the table. There is a smashing of glass. A tense pause; then suddenly a woman gives a wild hysterical scream and the restaurant springs to life*)

MARGARET: (*Staggered*) Oh … oh …

MARKHAM: What is it? What's … what's the matter with him …?

MARGARET: (*Softly*) He's dead … he's dead … (*Suddenly hysterical*) My God … it's murder …! Julius … Julius … It's murder!!!

FADE IN music.

Slow FADE DOWN of music.
FADE IN the voice of CAMPBELL MANSFIELD.

MANSFIELD: (*Excitedly bewildered*) Well … I mean to say … what … what a perfectly extraordinary story! But – but what actually happened when …

SHALE: When Julius Markham and Margaret Freeman realised that Leo was, without any question of … (*Suddenly*) Say, is … is that clock right?

MANSFIELD: M'm? Oh, yes! Yes … it's … about right!

SHALE: Chee, I'd no idea it was that late! I'd better be making a move. I've got an appointment down town at nine o'clock.

MANSFIELD: (*Anxiously*) Yes … Yes … but … but what happened? I mean to say … you can't just leave the story like this … I mean to say, it's … er … it's …

SHALE: (*Chuckling*) Well, supposing we meet here next week …?

MANSFIELD: The same time?

121

SHALE: Yes … Yes, rather! By all means! (*With an amused yet bewildered chuckle*)

It is nine o'clock. The cuckoo clock announces the hour.

Cuckoo! Cuckoo! Cuckoo! Cuckoo! Cuckoo! Cuckoo! Cuckoo! Cuckoo! Cuckoo!

END OF EPISODE FIVE

EPISODE SIX

BEVERLEY HILLS

OPEN TO:	Cuckoo! Cuckoo! Cuckoo! Cuckoo! Cuckoo! Cuckoo! Cuckoo! Cuckoo!

DALLAS SHALE arrives.

SHALE:	Hello, there! Am I late?
MANSFIELD:	No … No … Just on time. I've ordered you a drink.
SHALE:	Oh, swell.
CHARLIE:	(*Bringing the drinks*) One highball … one ginger ale.
SHALE:	Ginger ale? Say, what is this, Independence Day?
MANSFIELD:	(*Raising his glass*) Cheerio! (*After a tiny pause*) You … er … you were telling me about …
SHALE:	(*Suddenly*) Oh, yeah! Yeah! … Well, Oliver Hartington … in other words the Czar of Hollywood … was found mysteriously murdered in The Blue Stetson restaurant. It was early Tuesday morning when the murder was discovered, but in London, of course, it was still Monday evening – so the English newspapers brought out a special edition with the headline …
MANSFIELD:	Mr Hartington died tomorrow …
SHALE:	Yeah. Well, several days after Hartington was murdered Margaret Freeman, the actress, visited The Blue Stetson with her husband, or rather her ex-husband … Leo Bartlett. Julius Markham, the famous H.G.T. producer, crossed over to their table. Markham had more or less stepped into Mr Hartington's shoes and was none … (*FADE voice completely*)

FADE Scene.

FADE UP the scene at The Blue Stetson.
FADE IN of JULIUS MARKHAM.

MARKHAM: ... Oh, by the way, before I forget ... I want to see you tomorrow morning in my office ... about eleven-thirty ... (*Pleased with himself*) You ... know what it's about?

MARGARET: Yes, I think so, Julius ...

MARKHAM: We've paid a hundred thousand dollars for this story, Margaret, and ... (*After a slight pause*) What's the matter with your friend?

MARGARET: Oh, I'm sorry, my dear. (*Turning towards LEO*) Leo, I want you to meet Julius Markham our new ... Leo! ... Don't be silly ... wake up ...

MARKHAM: (*Laughing*) What's he trying to do ... impersonate Hartington? Is this some kind of an audition for ...

He stops speaking, and the moment he does so LEO falls forward across the table. There is a smashing of glass.
There is a tense pause; then suddenly a woman gives a wild hysterical scream and the restaurant springs to life.

MARGARET: (*Staggered*) Oh ... oh ...

MARKHAM: What is it? What's ... what's the matter with him ...?

MARGARET: (*Softly*) He's dead ... he's dead ... (*Suddenly hysterical*) My God ... it's murder ...! Julius ... Julius ... It's murder!!!

MARKHAM: (*Nervously: embarrassed*) For God's sake, Margaret!

SYLVESTOR: (*Arriving at the table*) What is it? What's the matter ...?

MARGARET: (*Bewildered: still hysterical*) He's dead ... Oh, my God! He's dead ... He's dead ... He's dead ...

126

MARKHAM: Margaret ... for God's sake ...

PETER arrives at the table. He is excited and rather breathless.

PETER: Send a waiter across to Joe's Place ... quickly!

SYLVESTOR: (*Surprised*) Joe's Place ...? What – what the devil are you talking about ...?

PETER: (*Taking command*) Do as I tell you!

SYLVESTOR: (*Puzzled*) But why ...?

PETER: O'Hara's there ... I promised to meet him when we closed, and ... (*Suddenly*) Stand away from the table, sir! (*To SYLVESTOR*) We need a screen round here ...

SYLVESTOR: (*Pulling himself together*) Yes ... Yes, all right. I'll ... Oh! Here's Lionel ... good ... he's got one!

PETER: Good! Now put the screen across ...

They move the screen into position.

PETER: That's it! Lionel ... you know Inspector O'Hara, the officer who was in charge the night ...

LIONEL: Sure ... I know O'Hara ...

PETER: Well, you'll find him across at Joe's Place ... fetch him over here ... tell him it's urgent!

SYLVESTOR: That's all right, Lionel.

LIONEL: O.K. ...

LIONEL departs.

MARGARET commences to weep ... she is hysterical and cannot control herself.

SYLVESTOR: (*Anxiously*) Miss Freeman ... please!

MARKHAM: For God's sake, Margaret ... pull yourself together!

MARGARET endeavours to control herself, but is unable to do so.

SYLVESTOR: Miss Freeman, do try and ...

PETER:	(*Quickly*) Here … hold these flowers! (*He grabs a vase*)
MARKHAM:	What – what are you going to do?
SYLVESTOR:	(*Anxiously*) There's a lot of water in that bowl, don't …

PETER empties the bowl of water all over MARGARET.

MARGARET:	(*Gasping for breath*) Oh! … Oh! … Oh! … Oh!
MARKHAM:	(*Laughing*) Gee … it's done the trick all right!
SYLVESTOR:	(*Apologetically*) Miss Freeman … Miss Freeman … I – I – I'm most terribly sorry I … I never thought for …
MARGARET:	Look – look at my dress! Just … Just look at it! Why … Why, you … (*She slaps SYLVESTOR across the face*)
MARKHAM:	(*Amused*) That's the wrong guy!
MARGARET:	(*Softly*) God, I feel awful! Get – get me a brandy …
MARKHAM:	Hello, who's this …?

DR LATIMER arrives. He is an Englishman.

PETER:	I beg your pardon, sir, but please …
DR LATIMER:	Can I be of any assistance at all? My name is Dr Latimer, I was in the cocktail bar and one of the waiters told me … that … (*He looks at LEO*) Hello! … Hello … What's this …?

There is a pause.

SYLVESTOR:	He's … He's dead?
DR LATIMER:	M'm … Yes, I'm afraid so. But – but how did this happen?
MARGARET:	(*Bewildered*) Well, we … we don't really know … He was sitting at the table quite normally and then …
MARKHAM:	(*Interrupting MARGARET: quietly*) What – what would you say was the cause of death?

128

DR LATIMER:	I wouldn't like to venture an opinion, not without an autopsy, but – er – speaking ... er ... quite ... off the record as it were ... there appears to be one or two indications of asphyxiation.
MARKHAM:	Asphyxiation ...?
DR LATIMER:	(*Thoughtfully*) Yes ...
SYLVESTOR:	(*Suddenly*) Here's the Inspector!

The voice of DIVISIONAL-INSPECTOR O'HARA can be heard. He arrives with GAIL HOWARD.

O'HARA:	Hello, Sylvestor! Say, what the hell goes on around here anyway?
PETER:	(*Surprised*) Gail ... what are you doing here?
GAIL:	(*Rather surprised by PETER's tone*) What do you mean? I was with O'Hara at Joe's Place; you said you'd join us when the restaurant closed and ...
PETER:	Yes, but you ought to have stayed there!
GAIL:	(*Puzzled*) Peter ... what's happened?
O'HARA:	(*Suddenly: taking complete command*) Where's the phone?
SYLVESTOR:	There's one in the vestibule, and there's one ...
O'HARA:	(*Briskly*) I want someone to get through to headquarters for me ...
SYLVESTOR:	I'll do it with pleasure.
O'HARA:	No, you stay here, Sylvestor! Miss Howard, get through to Plaza 1-1234. Ask for Sergeant Mallory – explain what's happened – and tell him I want Quinn, Symons, Dane and Ferdy ...
GAIL:	Quinn ... Symons ... Dane ... Ferdy ...
O'HARA:	Yeah ... Oh, an' tell Mallory it's urgent – so he'd better take the lead out of his pants!
GAIL:	(*Laughing*) Yes, all right ...

GAIL leaves.

O'HARA:	I'll need your office, Sylvestor.
SYLVESTOR:	It's at your disposal, Inspector.
O'HARA:	Good. Well, you might take Miss Freeman, Mr Markham, and this gentleman …
DR LATIMER:	Dr Latimer … I was in the cocktail bar when this happened, but one of the waiters told me that someone had been taken ill, so naturally …
O'HARA:	Sure … Sure … You stay behind, doctor.
MARKHAM:	(*Irritated*) Say, what's the idea, O'Hara? I've got a guest here – I can't just leave him high an' dry.
MARGARET:	If you've got any questions to ask, for God's sake, ask them now, and get it over with!
O'HARA:	Listen, Miss Freeman, time means nothing to me! If you get fresh I'll keep you here all night … remember that.
MARGARET:	(*Furiously*) Why, you cocky little squirt, I'll …
MARKHAM:	(*Quickly*) Margaret!!!

There is a pause while O'HARA stares at MARGARET.

O'HARA:	(*Quietly*) Take 'em up to the office …
SYLVESTOR:	(*Pouring oil on troubled waters*) Certainly, Inspector … Certainly! Er … this way, Miss Freeman … Mr Markham.
MARKHAM:	(*Annoyed: moving away*) I'll have to have a word with Schulberg.
MARGARET:	(*Moving away*) What about that brandy, Sylvestor?
SYLVESTOR:	I'll see to it myself, Miss Freeman.

A pause.

O'HARA:	Now we've got rid of the menagerie … you can spill the beans. What exactly happened?
PETER:	Well, I'm afraid there's not a great deal to tell, Inspector. They arrived about ten minutes ago

	and after a word or two with Sylvestor they were brought across to the table.
O'HARA:	Did you take their order?
PETER:	No. I'm afraid I was rather busy at the other end of the room.
O'HARA:	Did they seem quite friendly towards one another?
PETER:	Yes, I think so. He offered Miss Freeman a cigarette and then ...
DR LATIMER:	Did she take one?
PETER:	No – No, I don't think she did ... and then Markham came across. She turned to introduce Markham and ... well ... he just fell forward like this – across the table.
O'HARA:	M'm. (*He is searching LEO*) Cigarette case ... watch ... driving licence ... wallet ... Hello, what's this ... Oh ... Leo Bartlett, apartment 17 ... The Garden of Allah ... (*Thoughtfully*) M'm ... checked in this afternoon by the look of things. (*Suddenly: looking up*) What would you say was the cause of death?
DR LATIMER:	Quite frankly, I wouldn't like to venture an opinion – certainly not without a post-mortem.
PETER:	(*Quietly*) What made you ask about the cigarettes?
DR LATIMER:	About the cigarettes?
PETER:	Yes, you asked whether Miss Freeman took one or not.

A tiny pause.

| O'HARA: | Had you a reason for asking? |

A second pause.

| DR LATIMER: | (*Quietly*) Yes. I rather got the impression – after a very cursory examination, you understand – that he died from asphyxiation. |

131

	Then I noticed the cigarette he'd been smoking, and ...
O'HARA:	Cigarette? What's the matter with it?
DR LATIMER:	(*Cautiously*) Well, once again I'm afraid I shouldn't like to venture a professional opinion, not without first ...
O'HARA:	Yes – yes, but what do you think is the matter with it? Here ... here have a look at it!

There is a long pause.

O'HARA:	Well?
DR LATIMER:	I don't think any longer – I'm sure! Have you heard of Lokni?
O'HARA:	Lokni? Say, what's that, a patent medicine?
DR LATIMER:	No – it's a drug. In certain parts of the Dutch East Indies they smoke it instead of tobacco, but in small ... very small quantities.
O'HARA:	What effect does it have?
DR LATIMER:	On a person who is accustomed to smoking it – hardly any I should say. But on a person who isn't ... it might have pretty grave consequences.
O'HARA:	In your opinion ... is that what killed him?
DR LATIMER:	Well, I shouldn't like to go so far as ... er ... to say that. If he had a weak heart ... ah, yes! Yes, then I shouldn't ... I shouldn't hesitate.
O'HARA:	Is it an unpleasant smoke?
DR LATIMER:	No, no. I'm told it's just the opposite. As a matter of fact the local authorities did have quite a spot of bother at one time. Several of their own people rather got into the habit of ... Oh ... oh, well that's a long time ago.
O'HARA:	Sure! Can we get in touch with you, doctor, if by any ...

DR LATIMER: I shall be at The Waldorf Hotel until Tuesday, and then I leave for New York ... I'm sailing for New York on the 27th. My permanent address is 64B Wimpole Street ... London ... Dr Hugh C. Latimer.

O'HARA: (*Taking the particulars*) Dr ... Hugh ... C. Latimer ... (*Briskly*) Thank you, doctor! (*He replaces his book*) M'm ... Now we'll see what Margaret Freeman and the boyfriend have got to say, an' if they do a temperamental act I'll ... I'll mow 'em down!!!

PETER laughs.
FADE Scene.

CROSSFADE to SYLVESTOR's Office.
FADE UP of JULIUS MARKHAM. He is rather weary.

MARKHAM: If I've told you once I must have told you fifty times, I'd never even seen the guy before!

MARGARET: (*Irritated*) Julius simply came across to the table ... I turned to introduce him, and Leo fell forward ... that's – that's all that happened.

MARKHAM: Except that you went completely hay-wire!

MARGARET: Well, what the hell did you expect me to do ...? (*She is on the verge of tears*)

MARKHAM: Yes, o.k., Margaret. O.K!

O'HARA: Now let's kinda get this straight ... Leo Bartlett was your ex-husband ... he came to Hollywood about six months ago ... he was staying at The Garden of Allah ... and you were quite good friends ... Is that correct?

MARGARET: (*After a tiny pause*) Yes.

O'HARA: M'm.

MARKHAM: Inspector, I don't want to be awkward – I realise that you've got to go into details, but

133

	I've got a most important guest on my hands, and ...
O'HARA:	Can we reach you at the studios?
MARKHAM:	Certainly ... certainly ... all day tomorrow ... every day this week.
O'HARA:	(*After a slight hesitation*) O.K. ... you can go.
MARKHAM:	Thank you. Tomorrow morning, Margaret ... eleven-thirty ...

The door opens and closes.

O'HARA:	And now, Miss Freeman ...
MARGARET:	(*Angrily*) Say, listen! If Markham can go ... why can't I?
SYLVESTOR:	Miss Freeman, I'm sure the Inspector is merely ...
MARGARET:	(*Turning on SYLVESTOR*) You get the hell out of this an' mind your own blasted business!
O'HARA:	Now take it easy, lady! Take it ... easy!

The door opens and GAIL enters.

PETER:	Did you get through all right?
GAIL:	Yes. (*Amused*) Symons already here, Inspector, he's taking photographs.
O'HARA:	Good!
MARGARET:	I've – I've never been so humiliated in all my life! You bring me in here and treat me like a ... like a ...
O'HARA:	(*Politely*) A liar ...?
MARGARET:	(*Indignantly*) A liar ...? What – what do you mean?
SYLVESTOR:	(*Apologetically*) Inspector, I've – er – got one or two rather – er – important – er – matters which I'd like to ... er ...
O'HARA:	That's o.k., Sylvestor, I'll see you later.
SYLVESTOR:	Oh, er ... thank you, Inspector ... er ... Miss Freeman.

The door opens and closes as SYLVESTOR departs.

MARGARET: What – what do you mean by calling me a liar?

O'HARA: I didn't call you a liar, Miss Freeman – but I reckon the cap kinda fits. You see, in the first place, this guy Bartlett arrived in Hollywood this afternoon; he checked in at The Garden of Allah at about four-fifteen ... that's right, isn't it?

MARGARET: (*Suddenly changing her tactics: pleasantly*) Yes ... yes, I'm sorry, Inspector, I ought to have told you beforehand. I ... I don't really know why I didn't ... (*With a little laugh*) ... so silly of me. Leo arrived from New York this afternoon ... on the three-fifteen ... I met him at the station.

O'HARA: He lived in New York?

MARGARET: Oh, yes ... at least, for the past two or three years.

GAIL: (*Quietly*) Is that why his driving licence is issued by the State of Indiana?

PETER: What do you mean?

GAIL: This is his driving licence, isn't it?

O'HARA: Sure!

GAIL: Well, it's got his address on it ... naturally ... (*Reading*) "Leo Bartlett, Silver Springs, Nr. Indianapolis, Indiana ...!"

O'HARA: (*Bewildered*) Then what the hell ... (*Turning on MARGARET*) Say, are you deliberately trying to be funny with me, or ...

GAIL: (*Interrupting O'HARA*) Just a minute! (*Thoughtfully*) Indiana ... (*Suddenly*) Who is this man ... Leo Bartlett?

O'HARA: (*Perplexed*) What d'you mean ... who is he? He's the guy downstairs who's passed out!

135

GAIL: No … No … I mean, who …
MARGARET: (*Slowly*) Leo Bartlett was my husband, or
                 rather … my ex-husband. (*Suddenly*) What are
                 you trying to get at?
GAIL: What brought him to Hollywood, Miss
                 Freeman?

There is a pause.

O'HARA: (*Barking*) Go on … answer the question! What
                 brought the guy to Hollywood?
GAIL: (*Amused*) Do you know why I think Leo
                 Bartlett came to Hollywood? (*After a tiny
                 pause*) To impersonate Peter London …
PETER: (*Puzzled*) To impersonate me, but …
O'HARA: (*Suddenly*) Say, just a minute! There may be
                 something in this! Don't you remember that
                 cable that was …
GAIL: (*Quietly*) You sent for your husband, didn't
                 you? You instructed him to send that cable to
                 Hartington and then pretend to be Peter
                 London. When the real Peter London turned up
                 and Hartington was murdered, you …
MARGARET: (*Quickly: emotionally*) I tried to stop him … I
                 did my best to stop him … When he arrived
                 here I offered him five thousand dollars if he'd
                 return to Indiana … but he wouldn't.
GAIL: Why wouldn't he?
MARGARET: Because he was under the impression that by
                 staying in Hollywood he could make a great
                 deal more than five thousand dollars.
O'HARA: What at …? (*A pause*) What at!!!
MARGARET: (*Quietly*) Blackmail … (*After a tiny pause*) He
                 said that he knew … who'd murdered …
                 Hartington …
O'HARA: (*Staggered*) What!!!

PETER:	My God!
GAIL:	It looks as if he really did know!
O'HARA:	(*Softly*) Yeah ... (*After a tiny pause*) Miss Freeman, do you know who murdered Mr Hartington?
MARGARET:	(*Defiantly*) No!!!
O'HARA:	Or ... Mary Brampton?
MARGARET:	No!!!
O'HARA:	Or ... Leo Bartlett?
MARGARET:	No!!!

The door opens and SERGEANT DANE breaks into the room.

DANE:	We're all set downstairs ... anything else, Inspector?

There is a tiny pause.

O'HARA:	O.K. Sergeant – I'll be down in a minute.

FADE IN music.

FADE DOWN music.
CROSS FADE to a slight background of traffic.

FADE UP of a motor car which is travelling very slowly ... obviously climbing a very steep hill.

GAIL:	(*Amused*) It's a good job we're in no particular hurry ...
PETER:	Don't worry, she'll make it all right!
GAIL:	What happens if she falls to pieces?
PETER:	I lose the first instalment – but don't think of such things!
GAIL:	Is this the first time you've been up here?
PETER:	(*Amused*) No, I came up here the day I arrived in Hollywood ... I'd heard so much about this cock-eyed view I wanted to get a good look at it.
GAIL:	(*Laughing*) So did I!

PETER: Were you disappointed?

GAIL: No … I don't think so. After all, it is … pretty exciting, isn't it?

PETER: I'll pull into the kerb.

PETER draws the car to a standstill. The engine is switched off.

GAIL: What's that place? … No, over on the other side.

PETER: Oh, that's The Hollywood Bowl … Doesn't look quite so large from here, does it? (*After a tiny pause*) Cigarette?

GAIL: No, thank you.

PETER: What are you thinking of?

GAIL: I was just thinking of something I once read … about Hollywood, I mean.

PETER: (*Lighting his cigarette*) M'm … what was that?

GAIL: I just forget where I read it … it was in a magazine I think. Anyway, it said: "Hollywood is best described as a state of mind, for it can be all things to all men".

PETER: You've been reading some pretty high class magazines by the sound of things.

GAIL and PETER laugh.

A pause.

GAIL: Peter …

PETER: Yes?

GAIL: Do you think Margaret Freeman killed … Leo Bartlett?

PETER: (*Thoughtfully*) No … No, somehow … I don't think so.

GAIL: Who do you think did?

PETER: I don't know, but I've got a strong sort of feeling about Markham …

GAIL: Markham? No, I don't think Markham killed him – but one thing I am pretty sure about …

PETER: What's that …?

GAIL: I'm pretty sure that the person who killed Bartlett killed Mary Brampton and Mr Hartington.

PETER: (*Quietly*) Yes, I don't think there's any doubt about that. (*Suddenly*) Look here, I thought we came up here to admire the view! Let's forget about this Hartington business!

GAIL: I like the way we always call it the Hartington business.

PETER: Yes, well, it started with Hartington, and I'm fairly certain that the other two murders were only … (*Checking himself*) The view! The view, young lady!

PETER and GAIL laugh again.

GAIL: I think I will have that cigarette, after all.

PETER: Sure … (*He takes out his cigarette case*)

GAIL: Is this a lighter on the dashboard, Peter, or … (*Surprised*) Oh!

PETER: (*Amused*) It's a radio … Cigarette?

GAIL: Thank you.

The noise of dance music fades in from the radio …

PETER: You know this is a crazy sort of place. You see that red and white sign down there … no, the one that keeps turning round … yes, that's it! Do you know what it advertises?

GAIL: Coca-Cola?

PETER: No – it advertises a crematorium.

GAIL: No!

PETER: It does … honestly. (*Amused*) And just look at that other one … the sign that flickers …

GAIL: (*Peering*) What does it say …? (*Reading*) "We need … your heads … to run … our business …"

PETER: Yes – Pete's hairdressing salon …

GAIL: (*Laughing*) That's rather neat!

The dance orchestra on the radio stops.

PETER:	Quite the funniest advertisement I've ever seen was …
ANNOUNCER:	(*On the radio*) Attention, please! Attention, everybody!!!
GAIL:	What's this …?
PETER:	(*Quietly: fooling*) Do your teeth chatter with excitement? Have you spots before your eyes? Then take … (*He is interrupted by the voice from the radio*)
ANNOUNCER:	Hello, everybody … this is station KNX. Tonight by kind permission of The New York Daily Record and The Chicago Post, we bring you crime reporter No 1 … Henry K. Hammerston …
HAMMERSTON:	Just seventy-five minutes ago Leo Bartlett, ex-husband of Margaret Freeman, star of a dozen motion picture successes and twice runner-up for the Academy Award, was mysteriously murdered in The Blue Stetson restaurant on Sunset Boulevard, Hollywood. Since there can be little doubt that, in some mysterious way, this new outrage is connected with the murder of Mr Hartington, I have with me in the studio tonight – by kind permission of the H.G.T. Corporation – Miss Doris Charleston, confidential secretary and personal adviser to the late Oliver Hartington! Miss Charleston, tell me … how long did you work for Mr Hartington?
DORIS:	For nine years. I started work for the H.G.T. Corporation in December 1929. I … I was sixteen at the time.
HAMMERSTON:	Did you, during those nine years, ever come into personal contact with Mr Bartlett?

140

DORIS:	I have a vague recollection of meeting him at a party two or three years ago – but that's all.
HAMMERSTON:	Did Mr Hartington give the party?
DORIS:	No, it was given by a scenario writer … Dallas Shale. (*Faintly amused*) Mr Hartington never gave parties.
HAMMERSTON:	Was Leo Bartlett connected with the film industry at all?
DORIS:	Not to my knowledge. He certainly wasn't associated with H.G.T.
HAMMERSTON:	When Mr Hartington died, Ralph Ferguson – my worthy colleague on The New York Mail – suggested that it might quite possibly be suicide and not murder. The police of course have now definitely decided that it was murder, and recent events have certainly justified this – er – point of view … nevertheless, what is your re-action to the suggestion of suicide? Was Mr Hartington in good health?
DORIS:	(*Faintly amused*) He suffered, rather violently, from dyspepsia.
HAMMERSTON:	(*Softly: serious*) Stick to the script please!
DORIS:	No … Mr Hartington, so far as I know, was in perfect health.
PETER:	Shall I switch off?
GAIL:	No, wait a minute!
HAMMERSTON:	Miss Charleston, did you come into contact with Mary Brampton at all? The girl who was found murdered in an apartment house on …
DORIS:	Sure … quite frequently.
HAMMERSTON:	Did Mary Brampton work for Mr Hartington at any time?
DORIS:	Yes, once … for about a fortnight.

HAMMERSTON: Now, Miss Charleston, speaking quite frankly, and expressing a perfectly unbiased opinion, would you have said that Mr Hartington was a popular sort of person?

DORIS: (*Reading from her script*) Oh, yes ... Mr Hartington had a great personal charm and he was always so ... (*Rather surprised by what she is reading*) ... so kind and generous, he was in fact one of the best loved personalities in ... (*Suddenly, flaring up*) Say, who wrote this string of baloney? Of all the tenth-rate crap this takes the prize ...

GAIL: (*Amused*) What's happened?

PETER: Listen!

DORIS: ... Hartington was a heel – d'you follow me, Mr Hammerston ... he was a heel ... an' a phoney heel into the bargain! He was so god-darned crooked that even when he pulled the wool over your eyes it was half cotton! An' there's another point too brother, while we're on the subject ... he was greedy! Yeah ... greedy! The great Mr Hartington was greedy!!!

HAMMERSTON: (*Surprised*) You – you didn't like Mr Hartington, Miss Charleston?

DORIS: Like him? Listen brother – I don't know who gave Hartington the works, but one thing I do know ... it was a swell idea!!! (*Quietly: after a pause*) Goodnight.

HAMMERSTON: (*Excitedly*) Goodnight, Miss Charleston, an' many thanks for an interesting interview!

ANNOUNCER: (*FADING IN quickly*) ... You have been listening to Henry K. Hammerston, broadcasting to you through the courtesy of The New York Daily Record and …

The radio set is switched off.

GAIL:	Well – what do you think of that?
PETER:	(*Quietly*) I don't know what to think of it.
GAIL:	She sounded to me rather as if she had a grievance of some sort.
PETER:	Yes. (*Suddenly*) Oh, my God! Which ever way we turn we seem to run into this Hartington affair! Let's forget about it, Gail, if only for an hour or so.
GAIL:	Yes … all right.

A tiny pause.

PETER:	Comfy?
GAIL:	M'm – m'm. (*Casually; after a pause*) What's that place?
PETER:	Where?
GAIL:	On the right.
PETER:	Oh, Lord … there we go again!
GAIL:	(*Amused*) What is it?
PETER:	(*Laughing – in spite of himself*) It's the H.G.T. studios.
GAIL:	I'm sorry, Peter!

A pause.

PETER:	(*Seriously*) Gail … do you intend to stay in Hollywood?
GAIL:	What do you mean … indefinitely …?
PETER:	Yes.
GAIL:	That's rather difficult to say. Why do you ask?
PETER:	(*Hesitatingly*) I had a word with O'Hara tonight before we left The Blue Stetson and …
GAIL:	Yes, I saw you. (*Puzzled*) You seemed very intent, Peter … what were you talking about?

143

PETER: About you. Gail ... there's no necessity for you to
            remain in Hollywood just ... just because of this
            Hartington business.
GAIL: What do you mean? Don't you want me to stay in
            Hollywood?
PETER: (*Quietly*) No.
GAIL: Why not?
PETER: (*After a pause*) Because ... I'm in love with you – and
            because I know only too well what Hollywood can
            mean ... to a person in love.
GAIL: (*Softly*) I've got to stay here, Peter.
PETER: Why?
GAIL: Oh ... because of what Julius Markham once said,
            and a little man called Joe Francino ...
PETER: They said that you'd never make good in Hollywood,
            is that it?
GAIL: M'm – m'm ... I'm sorry, Peter, but do try and ...
            (*Suddenly: after a slight hesitation*) What's the matter
            with that car?
PETER: It's going all over the place! Why ... Good God! ...
            the man's drunk ...
*In the background the sound of a car can be heard. Suddenly,
with a grinding of brakes it commences to skid ...*
GAIL: He's going to bump into us!
PETER: No! No ... it's all right! My God, what a skid!!!
GAIL: Peter!!!
PETER: Hold tight!
The car skids to a standstill.
GAIL and PETER heave a sigh of relief.
The car door opens and closes.
GAIL: (*Surprised: quietly*) Look! Peter ... look! ... it's
            Louis Cheyne ...
PETER: Louis Cheyne?

GAIL: Yes ... the scenario writer ... you remember, he came to The Blue Stetson with Julius Markham and Doris Charleston the night Hartington ...

PETER: Yes ... Yes, of course. My word, he's pretty far gone, isn't he?

GAIL: (*Quietly*) He's coming over here ...

After a slight pause, LOUIS CHEYNE arrives. He is very inebriated, but extremely pleased with life – indeed, just at the moment he finds life extremely amusing.

LOUIS: Say, I'm frightfully sorry scaring the life out of ... of ... Hello, there! It's ... It's Peter London!!! How are you, Pete, old boy ... old boy ... old boy ...

PETER: Hello, Mr Cheyne ...

LOUIS: You remember me ...? Now isn't that nice ... Now ... isn't ... that ... nice ...

GAIL: I should drive your car into the side, Mr Cheyne – we'll take you back to town.

LOUIS: (*Suddenly*) Hello!!! (*Laughing*) I – I didn't see you! Gosh, but you're pretty ... isn't she pretty, Pete ... old boy?

PETER: (*Quietly*) I think so.

LOUIS: Gosh, but you're pretty ... pretty as a picture. (*Quickly*) Not an H.G.T. picture! Oh, my God – no! (*He shudders at the thought*) Brr!!!

PETER: (*Amused*) Jump in the car, Mr Cheyne – we'll drive you back.

LOUIS: No hurry ... No hurry, old boy ... Came up here to admire the view ... you see that pano ...panorama, Miss ... Miss ...?

GAIL: Howard.

LOUIS: Miss Howard ... it's Hollywood. Hollywood ... Naked and unashamed ... city of celluloid and glamour. Baloney and Ballyhoo ...

PETER: Come on, old man ... jump in the car.

145

LOUIS:	I'm all right ... don't worry ... I'm all right. (*Suddenly*) Let's have some music! Yes ... why not? ... let's have some music.
GAIL:	I'll turn the radio on.
LOUIS:	You two think that I'm pretty well cockeyed ... don't you? (*Laughing*) Well ... well, I am! An' who cares ...? Who cares?

The radio fades through. A dance band finishes.

ANNOUNCER:	This is Station KNX – stand by everybody for an important newsflash from Hollywood, California ...
2nd ANNOUNCER:	(*Quickly; excitedly*) Margaret Freeman, top-line star of the H.G.T. studios and twice runner-up for The Academy Award, has been arrested for the murder of Oliver Hartington! This information was given to our special representative in Los Angeles at ... (*The voices continue but cannot be heard distinctly because of GAIL, PETER and LOUIS...*)
GAIL:	(*Staggered*) Peter! Peter ... did you hear that ...? They've – they've arrested Margaret Freeman ...
PETER:	(*Bewildered*) Margaret ... Freeman!!!
LOUIS:	(*Amused: but surprised*) Now ... what do you know about that?

Suddenly LOUIS commences to laugh. He is laughing quite uproariously when ...
FADE IN music.

FADE DOWN music.
FADE IN the voice of CAMPBELL MANSFIELD.

146

MANSFIELD: You know, Shale, this – er – this story really – er
            – quite takes my breath away. I mean to say, why
            arrest Margaret Freeman? Surely O'Hara didn't
            …

SHALE: Well, O'Hara kinda figured that … (*Suddenly*)
            Now just look at that clock! Chee, how time
            flies!

MANSFIELD: (*Quickly*) Have another … er … er … highball?

SHALE: Sorry, I've got an appointment down town at
            nine o'clock. Say … supposing we meet here
            next week … the same time … the same place?

MANSFIELD: Yes – Yes, rather. By all means … (*With his
            amused, yet bewildered chuckle*) I mean to say
            …

The cuckoo clock announces the hour.

            Cuckoo! Cuckoo! Cuckoo! Cuckoo! Cuckoo!
            Cuckoo! Cuckoo! Cuckoo! Cuckoo!

END OF EPISODE SIX

EPISODE SEVEN

THE REMARKABLE BEHAVIOUR OF OTTO STULTZ

OPEN TO: Cuckoo! Cuckoo! Cuckoo! Cuckoo!
                Cuckoo! Cuckoo! Cuckoo! Cuckoo!
A second clock chimes the hour.

DALLAS SHALE arrives.

SHALE: Hello, there! Am I late?

MANSFIELD: (*Laughing*) No later than usual, Mr Shale! I've ordered you a drink.

SHALE: And I can use it!

MANSFIELD: (*Raising his glass*) Cheerio!

SHALE: Skoal! (*After drinking*) Now let's see … where did I get to – with the story, I mean?

MANSFIELD: Well, you told me that Gail Howard, Peter London and Louis Cheyne suddenly heard over the radio that Margaret Freeman had been arrested for the murder of Mr Hartington.

SHALE: Yeah – that's right! Well, you can imagine the sort of sensation that caused in Hollywood! Boy, the whole place was in an uproar! The morning after the night Margaret was arrested Julius Markham had arranged to meet Margaret in his office, in order to discuss her part in the new H.G.T. epic The Sky Is Always Dark. Markham had taken over Carnegie Hall, or in other words Mr Hartington's office, and at about eleven thirty I strolled out of a nearby conference room and made my way towards … (*FADE voice completely*)

FADE scene.

A knock is heard and a door opens.

MARKHAM: (*Extremely on edge, worried, and irritated*) Hello, Shale … What the devil do you want?

SHALE: I'd like to have a word with Doris.

MARKHAM:	She's in the other office.
SHALE:	O.K.
MARKHAM:	(*After a tiny pause*) Oh, Shale …
SHALE:	Yes …?
MARKHAM:	Did you hear the broadcast last night?
SHALE:	(*Amused*) M'm – m'm.
MARKHAM:	What the hell was Doris playing at?
SHALE:	(*Laughing*) She certainly spilt the beans about Hartington.
MARKHAM:	Yeah – swell publicity we're getting these days!
SHALE:	Say, what's going to happen about Margaret?
MARKHAM:	God knows!
SHALE:	Is she out on …
MARKHAM:	(*Interrupting SHALE*) Yeah – I'm expecting her any minute.
SHALE:	You know, Markham, the boys aren't too happy about this Horace Wyndham Harringford's story … The Sky is Always Dark.
MARKHAM:	What d'you mean – not happy about it? We didn't pay a hundred thousand dollars to make the scenario department happy! We paid a hundred thousand dollars because it's a swell story!
SHALE:	Yes, the story's o.k. … if you like that sort of thing. But quite frankly we … well, we just can't see Margaret in the part.
MARKHAM:	What is this, a conspiracy? Otto Stultz said exactly the same!!

A buzzer is heard – the click of a dictograph.

MARKHAM:	Yeah?
DORIS:	(*From the dictograph*) Mr Horace Wyndham Harringford has arrived.

152

MARKHAM:	Send him up … Oh, an' say – where have you put my dyspepsia tablets, I can't find the darn things anywhere!
DORIS:	I haven't seen 'em.
MARKHAM:	(*Sarcastically*) Well, if it's not too much trouble. Miss Charleston, would you mind having a look for 'em?
DORIS:	(*Unruffled*) Sure – it's a pleasure.

The dictograph is switched off.

SHALE:	Horace Wyndham Harringford …? He's the author of The Sky is Always Dark.
MARKHAM:	Sure.
SHALE:	Well … what's he doing in Hollywood?
MARKHAM:	(*Faintly exasperated*) What d'you mean … what's he doing in Hollywood? He's over here to help you boys script the novel …
SHALE:	You mean … he's going to attend all our script conferences?
MARKHAM:	Certainly! He wouldn't part with the film rights – except on that condition.
SHALE:	The hundred thousand, I take it, was just a side issue? What's he like?
MARKHAM:	(*Slightly puzzled*) Well, I've only spoken to him over the phone – I had a hell of a game understanding the guy.
SHALE:	What is he … an Eskimo?
MARKHAM:	I rather gather he's a Scotsman – there seemed to be a hell of a lot of "Och-ayes" floating around in the conversation.

There is a knock and the door opens.

DORIS:	Mr Horace Wyndham Harringford.

The door closes. Mr HORACE WYNDHAM HARRINGFORD is indeed a Scotsman. He is by no means easy to understand.

H.W.H.:	Mr Markham, I take it? I'm verra pleased to meet you, Mr Markham!
MARKHAM:	Glad to meet you too, Mr Harringford. This is Mr Dallas Shale – Mr Shale is attached to our scenario department.
SHALE:	How'd you do, Mr Harringford?
H.W.H.:	I'm verra pleased to meet you, Mr Whale.
SHALE:	Shale …
H.W.H.:	Mr Shale. (*Feeling the heat*) D'you mind if I take this coat off, Mr Markham?
MARKHAM:	Not at all.
H.W.H.:	(*Removing his coat*) Tha e blath.
SHALE:	I beg your pardon?
H.W.H.:	Tha e blath … Oh, I was forgetting, I don't suppose ye speak Gaelic?
SHALE:	(*Pulling H.W.H's leg*) Very indifferently …
H.W.H.:	I was just saying … it's very warm.
MARKHAM:	(*Puzzled*) It's very … Oh! Sure! Sure!
SHALE:	Will you have a cigarette?
H.W.H.:	Thank ye, but I never smoke. Now, Mr Markham, if you've no objection I'd like to get down to brass tacks.
MARKHAM:	I beg your pardon?
H.W.H.:	I said … I'd like to get down to brass tacks.
MARKHAM:	You'd like to … Oh, yeah! Yeah … I see what you mean.
H.W.H.:	I want to speak to you about Miss Freeman … Miss Margaret Freeman …
MARKHAM:	Yeah …?
H.W.H.:	Is it your intention now that she should play Charlotte Early in my story The Sky is Always Dark …?
MARKHAM:	Yeah … that's – er – that's what we've got in mind.

SHALE:	Don't you approve of the suggestion?
H.W.H.:	I think it's the most rantipole suggestion I've ever heard in my life!
MARKHAM:	(*To SHALE*) What is this ... Gaelic?
SHALE:	He doesn't like the idea.
MARKHAM:	He doesn't like the ... (*The great film magnate*) Mr Harringford, Miss Margaret Freeman is the greatest dramatic actress Hollywood has had ...
H.W.H.:	(*Interrupting MARKHAM*) I don't want a publicity blurb, an' I don't want a boost for the young lady. I'm simply telling ye that so far as playing the part of Charlotte Early is concerned – I won't hear of it!
MARKHAM:	(*Staggered*) You won't ... hear of it?
H.W.H.:	(*Completely unruffled*) That's what I said ...
MARKHAM:	(*After a pause: weakly*) Shale ... Shale, get me a glass of water.
SHALE:	Sure.
H.W.H.:	(*Politely*) Is it the heat you're feeling, Mr Markham?
SHALE:	(*From the other side of the room*) Yeah – an' you kind of turned it on, brother! (*He chuckles*)

The door opens.

DORIS:	There's a call from Philadelphia for Mr Harringford – A Mr Belmost of The Saturday Evening Post.
H.W.H.:	Oh, yes ... I'm expecting it; d'you think I might possibly ...
SHALE:	Mr Harringford can take the call in my office, Doris.
H.W.H.:	Thank ye, Mr Shale, I'm greatly obliged ...
DORIS:	This way ...
H.W.H.:	Thank ye ...

The door closes.

155

MARKHAM:	Shale … Shale, did you hear that crazy guy!!!
SHALE:	(*Quietly*) Yeah … Yeah, I heard him.
MARKHAM:	(*Bewildered: repeating Harringford's words*) "I'm simply telling ye that so far as playing the part of Charlotte Early is concerned – I won't hear of it!!" He won't hear of it!!! Who – who the hell does he think he is … that guy?
SHALE:	Here … drink this.

MARKHAM drinks.

MARKHAM:	Of all the God darn nerve! Why for two pins I'd …
SHALE:	(*Interrupting MARKHAM*) He's a funny little cove, an' kinda hard to understand … but you know, Markham, he's right …
MARKHAM:	What d'you mean … he's right?
SHALE:	About Margaret … She's no more my idea of Charlotte Early than I'm … Scarlett O'Hara.
MARKHAM:	(*Impetuously: yet weakening*) But – but if we don't use Margaret who … who the hell can we use?
SHALE:	That's your headache …
MARKHAM:	Vivien Leigh would be swell but she's all tied up with …

The door opens.

MARKHAM:	What is it?
DORIS:	Miss Freeman's here … She'd like to see you straight away, if possible.
MARKHAM:	O.K. … an' for God's sake find me those dyspepsia tablets!
SHALE:	I'll take Harringford down an' introduce him to the boys …
MARKHAM:	I don't care what you do with him, but keep the sunnavabitch out of my hair!
SHALE:	(*Laughing*) O.K!

MARKHAM:	(*Suddenly*) Margaret! Margaret, my dear … come in!
MARGARET:	Hello, Julius! My God, I've had a time of it …
MARKHAM:	Sit down, Margaret! Sit down … I'll get you a drink.
MARGARET:	No. No, I'm o.k. …
MARKHAM:	But what happened … last night, I mean?
MARGARET:	They took me down to headquarters and put me through a sort of third degree – My God, it was awful, Julius … Talk! Talk! I've never heard anything like it.
MARKHAM:	(*Puzzled*) Talk! What did they talk about?
MARGARET:	What the hell do you think they talked about … the weather?
MARKHAM:	But I thought they arrested you? Didn't you confess?
MARGARET:	Confess? What about? (*Suddenly*) Good God, Julius, you don't think I killed Hartington!
MARKHAM:	No. No, of course not; but when they announced over the radio that you'd been arrested I naturally …
MARGARET:	That was a bluff. Not a very smart one either – I think O'Hara had a crazy sort of idea that as soon as that was announced the real murderer would make a dash for it. They've been watching every way out of town since eleven o'clock last night.
MARKHAM:	But what's the position – so far as you're concerned?
MARGARET:	Oh, I'm all right – I'm quite free to do as I please.
MARKHAM:	They've released you?
MARGARET:	(*Rather surprised at MARKHAM's attitude*) Of course they've released me! (*Pleasantly*) I'm

	ready for work, Julius – In fact work is just what I need. It'll take my mind off things. You wanted to see me about the part of Charlotte Early in The Sky is Always Dark, didn't you?
MARKHAM:	M'm. (*Suddenly*) Oh, yes, Margaret, that's right ... the part of Charlotte Early.
MARGARET:	It's a lovely story, Julius, and a swell part.
MARKHAM:	Yes ... Yes, I believe so.
MARGARET:	(*Surprised*) Why, haven't you read it?
MARKHAM:	No. No, I'm afraid I haven't. I've been kind of busy just recently and ... (*After a pause*) Margaret, do you think the part is really ... really ...
MARGARET:	Really ... what?
MARKHAM:	Really suitable for you?
MARGARET:	Why of course it's suitable for me! It's a lovely part – I've already said so.
MARKHAM:	I don't know. It seems to me kinda young ...
MARGARET:	What do you mean kind of young?
MARKHAM:	Well, Charlotte's only supposed to be sixteen or seventeen at the beginning you know, and then she's a girl of about twenty-two, and then ...
MARGARET:	You're telling me, and I've read the book! Say, look here, Julius, what the hell are you getting at?
MARKHAM:	(*Quietly*) Now take it easy, Margaret! Take it easy!
A tiny pause.	
MARGARET:	(*Quietly*) You don't want me to play the part, do you?
MARKHAM:	Well ...
MARGARET:	Do you ...?

MARKHAM:	It isn't a question of what I want, Margaret, it's …
MARGARET:	(*Angrily*) Don't stall, Julius! For Pete's sake don't stall! You either want me to play the part, or you don't want me to play it.
MARKHAM:	Well, if you must know, it's Stultz. He doesn't think that you'd be any good.
MARGARET:	(*Surprised*) Stultz!!! Why – Why, is he going to direct the picture?
MARKHAM:	He is.
MARGARET:	(*Staggered*) Stultz … Otto Stultz …? Julius, you're not serious?
MARKHAM:	Of course I'm serious!
MARGARET:	For crying out loud!!! What the hell does Stultz know about it? Why he's nothing better than a Chief Nodder.
MARKHAM:	Now don't be silly, Margaret, we mustn't be prejudiced; after all, Otto did direct …
MARGARET:	Listen, Julius! Listen! There's more in this than meets the eye. Why doesn't Otto want me to play the part of Charlotte Early – that's what I want to know?
MARKHAM:	Because …
MARGARET:	Well?
MARKHAM:	Because of all this publicity about Hartington. Publicity is all very well, if it's the right kind of publicity, Margaret.
MARGARET:	Publicity! What the hell do you mean, publicity? D'you think I got a kick out of being arrested! D'you think it was my idea of fun spending the night with a half-a-dozen flat-feet?
MARKHAM:	Oh, you've had a tough time of it, Margaret. I know – an' I sympathise!

159

MARGARET:	Sympathise – to hell! Listen, Julius, I want to play the part of Charlotte Early and I've made up my mind that I'm going to play the part of Charlotte Early, because if I don't – well – I shouldn't like to be Otto Stultz ... that's all.
MARKHAM:	(*Softly: surprised*) Say ... Say, are you threatening Otto?

A tiny pause.

Suddenly MARGARET laughs.

MARGARET:	(*Sweetly*) Now don't be silly, Julius. I'm going home to bed, darling. I certainly need some sleep after last night. If you want me, Julius, for anything you ... er ... you know where I'll be. Goodbye, darling!

The door opens and closes.

The dictograph buzzer is heard. MARKHAM knocks the switch down.

MARKHAM:	Yeah?
DORIS:	(*From the dictograph*) There's a girl out here, she says that she'd like to see you ... a Miss Howard ...
MARKHAM:	I'm busy! And for goodness sake find those dyspepsia tablets!!!
DORIS:	(*Wearily*) O.K.
MARKHAM:	(*Suddenly*) Say, just a minute ... Miss Howard did you say? Is that the girl who pretended to be Peter London?
DORIS:	M'm – m'm ...
MARKHAM:	What does she want?
DORIS:	(*Mechanically*) She ... says ... she wants to see you ...
MARKHAM:	Yeah ... yeah, but what about?
DORIS:	(*Puzzled*) I don't get it ... She says it's about a pot of jam.

MARKHAM:	A pot of jam! (*Suddenly amused*) O.K., send her in, Doris. (*He knocks down the switch then lifts a telephone receiver*) Beverley? ... Markham here ... Listen, don't do anything about those dresses ... yeah ... the ones for Miss Freeman ... No, I'll let you know ... Well, you'll have to hold him off for a day or two! ... O.K. (*He replaces the receiver*)

During the telephone conversation the door has opened and GAIL has entered the office.

GAIL:	(*Pleasantly*) Good morning ...
MARKHAM:	Good morning; an' what do you want?
GAIL:	Mr Markham, do you remember when I stopped you one day ... in the outer office?
MARKHAM:	Sure! Sure!
GAIL:	You told me that so far as you film people are concerned, we Beauty Contest girls are just so many pots of jam, and that when you're ready ...
MARKHAM:	When we're ready for you we'll take you off the shelf. Sure, I remember!
GAIL:	Well, correct me if I'm mistaken, Mr Markham, but it seems to me that, so far as this particular pot of jam is concerned, you're ready for me!
MARKHAM:	I don't get this?
GAIL:	Shall I come to the point?
MARKHAM:	(*Irritated*) If you don't come to the point young lady, you'll mighty soon be talking to yourself!
GAIL:	H.G.T. have bought the film rights of a story called The Sky is Always Dark by Horace Wyndham Harringford.
MARKHAM:	Correct!

161

GAIL:	The principal character in the story is a girl called Charlotte Early.
MARKHAM:	Correct!
GAIL:	Well ... I want to play the part of Charlotte Early ... (*Almost an afterthought*) ... please.
MARKHAM:	You ... You want to play the part of ... Charlotte Early ...? (*Suddenly he roars with laughter*)
GAIL:	Why are you laughing?
MARKHAM:	Why am I laughing!!! Why am I ... (*He is almost speechless*) The audacity of the girl!!! The sheer audacity!!! Don't you realise ... Don't you realise that every actress in Hollywood ... every actress in America wants to play the part of Charlotte Early!!!
GAIL:	(*Politely*) What about the men?
MARKHAM:	What about ... (*Suddenly*) Say, are you trying to be funny?
GAIL:	Mr Markham, I'm going to offer you a proposition.
MARKHAM:	You're going to offer me a proposition!
GAIL:	That's right. Have you read the story of The Sky is Always Dark?
MARKHAM:	No – but my scenario department have made a synopsis of it, I know what it's all about.
GAIL:	Good. You know for instance that Charlotte is supposed to be a girl of about sixteen or seventeen to start with – and then a girl of about twenty-two, and then a woman of about thirty.
MARKHAM:	That's right!
GAIL:	Well – take a good look at me.
MARKHAM:	What d'you mean – take a good look at you?
GAIL:	Take a good look at me!

A pause.
MARKHAM is looking at GAIL.

MARKHAM: M'm ...

GAIL: Well?

MARKHAM: Not bad ... Not bad.

GAIL: How old do I look?

MARKHAM: Twenty-two ... twenty-three ...

GAIL: I'm twenty-four. And I can look seventeen if I want to, and I can look twenty-two, and I can look thirty – in fact, Mr Markham, I can look exactly like Charlotte Early should look, but probably won't, if you cast someone like Margaret Freeman for the part.

MARKHAM: You're crazy!

GAIL: Supposing I play the part of Charlotte and I make a success of it – what are people going to say?

MARKHAM: It's a miracle!

GAIL: They're going to say, who is this girl? Where does she come from? And who found her? And the answer to that is going to be ... she was discovered by Julius Markham, the new head of the H.G.T. Corporation.

MARKHAM: M'm – that's not bad! Maybe you've got something! Maybe you've got something at that!

GAIL: How long would it take you to arrange a test?

MARKHAM: Arrange a test? We can do that almost anytime.

GAIL: Then supposing we say this afternoon at three-thirty, is that all right?

MARKHAM: This afternoon at ... (*Suddenly*) Say, what the hell are you trying to do, run this organisation?

163

GAIL: (*Pleasantly*) Well, I can hardly expect you to
                        hand over the part without at least a test ...
                        three-thirty, Mr Markham ... o.k.?
MARKHAM: I'll – I'll think about it!
GAIL: (*Laughing*) Thanks.
The door closes.
There is a pause.
MARKHAM: (*Thoughtfully to himself*) They're going to say
                        ... Who is this girl? Where does she come
                        from? And who found her? And the answer to
                        that is going to be Julius Markham ... Julius
                        Markham, the new head of the H.G.T.
                        corporation ... Not bad. Not bad at all. (*He lifts
                        the telephone receiver*) Hello ...? Hello ...
                        Schooner? ... Markham here ... I want a test
                        this afternoon ... Three-thirty ... Yeah ...
                        Yeah, o.k. ... Oh an' Schooner ... you'd better
                        make it good ... real good! ... Get me? ... O.K.
                        ... (*He replaces the receiver*)
FADE Scene.
FADE IN music.
FADE DOWN.

FADE UP of cafeteria noises.
MAN: Get your tray at the other end, please! Move
                        along, sir ... no, you'll get your ticket at the
                        end, sir ... Move along ... Keep moving, Miss
                        ...
*GAIL arrives; she is very pleased with herself and obviously
excited.*
GAIL: (*Shouting*) Peter! Peter!!!
PETER: Oh, there you are! I'll be with you in a second!
                        Try and find a table!
GAIL: Yes, all right!

A pause.
PETER joins GAIL at the table.

PETER: Well, is this all right? Cold chicken ... salad ... and some apple pie ...

GAIL: Lovely! Sit down darling, I'm far too excited to eat anything!

PETER: I gather the test was a success?

GAIL: Yes ... Yes, I think it was.

PETER: I'll get some coffee.

GAIL: No. No, do sit down, Peter.

PETER: (*Laughing*) My word, you are excited!

GAIL: I really don't know whether I'm on my head or my heels. (*Amused*) It's exactly like a ... a sort ... of dream!

PETER: What happened exactly?

GAIL: What didn't happen! Halfway through the test Margaret Freeman walked on to the set ... She looked absolutely livid! I really felt quite sorry for Markham, the poor little devil didn't know where to put himself!

PETER: Did Markham say anything?

GAIL: About the test? Yes – yes, he was quite pleasant. As a matter of fact, I think he was rather surprised. (*Laughing*) I rather surprised myself to be quite honest!

PETER: Do you think you'll get the part?

GAIL: (*Thoughtfully*) I don't know ... (*Brightly*) Although, I must confess, I feel quite optimistic.

PETER: Well, that's something anyway ... Chicken?

GAIL: Thanks. No ... No dressing, darling ... I know one thing, I wouldn't like to be in Markham's shoes if ... Oh, thanks!

PETER: If what ...?

GAIL: If I do get the part ...

PETER: Why do you say that?

GAIL:	(*Thoughtfully*) She's a funny person … Margaret Freeman … I don't think she'd stop at anything, if she thought that Markham had more or less double-crossed her. He did promise her the part of Charlotte Early, there's no doubt about that.
PETER:	Yes, well, she may get it yet – you never know.
GAIL:	Oh, don't say that, darling – please!

A tiny pause.

PETER:	Gail …
GAIL:	Yes?
PETER:	Do you think Margaret Freeman … murdered Mr Hartington?
GAIL:	(*Thoughtfully*) I don't know. I think she'd be capable of it.
PETER:	(*Suddenly*) I saw O'Hara this morning for about half an hour.
GAIL:	Oh, yes?
PETER:	He didn't say a great deal, but it seemed to me he was pretty excited about something. Sugar?
GAIL:	Thanks.
PETER:	You know, he's got a theory … O'Hara … and a rather interesting one too. He's no longer convinced that Mr Hartington, Mary Brampton and Margaret Freeman's ex-husband Leo Bartlett were murdered by the same person.
GAIL:	(*Surprised*) But they must have been murdered by the same person, Peter!
PETER:	Not necessarily! Supposing, for instance, someone murdered Mr Hartington called X and Mary Brampton thought that Mr Hartington had been murdered by a person called Y. Now Y might be a fairly desperate sort of person with an extremely good motive for murdering Hartington. If the police discovered this, things would look pretty

black for Y, so Y gets rid of Mary Brampton – but that doesn't necessarily mean that Y murdered Mr Hartington in the first place.

GAIL: (*Amused*) That seems very involved, Peter!

PETER: I don't know … (*Thoughtfully*) I think maybe O'Hara's right … one person didn't murder Mr Hartington, Mary Brampton, and Leo Bartlett … I'm pretty sure about that now …

GAIL: Well, have some apple pie!

PETER: (*Laughing*) I can see you're in no mood for theories!

GAIL: Let's go to a movie! There's an awfully good one over at the Matamount.

PETER: Yes. O.K. … (*Suddenly, after a pause*) Oh, and Gail …

GAIL: Yes …?

PETER: There's – there's something … I want to tell you.

GAIL: Yes …?

PETER: You remember last night when we went out in the car together and … and … well … I sounded rather despondent about things … well … I've changed my mind.

GAIL: What do you mean … changed your mind, Peter? About what …?

PETER: About Hollywood … I'm going to stick it here … I'm going to beat this cock-eyed, one-sided, nickel-plated funfair at its own game!

GAIL: (*Delighted*) That's the idea!

PETER: And – And there's another thing too, Gail … If you do get the part of Charlotte Early, and if you do make good at it – don't think I'm going to walk out on you just because you'll be a star and I'll be a nonentity! Oh, no! Oh, no little girl! That situation might be all right for Tyrone Power in a

167

five hundred thousand dollar movie – but it's no good for Peter London in real life. No, sir – You make good in the part of Charlotte Early, and I'll marry you. I'll marry you, Gail Howard, if ... if ... if it's the last God darn thing I do!!!

GAIL: (*Both amused, and rather sentimentally touched*) Why, Mr London ... have some more apple pie ...

FADE In music.
CROSSFADE to quick exciting music.

FADE DOWN for voices.

JANE: (*American*) Hello, there! This is Jane Wise, your favourite Hollywood reporter. Gail Howard, twenty-four-year-old Beauty Contest Queen, snatches the part of the year – Charlotte Early in the new H.G.T. epic The Sky is Always Dark. Nice work, Miss Howard – if you can get it!!!

2nd VOICE: Variety!!! Flash!!! H.G.T. hand Freeman the frozen mitt ... Beauty Queen takes Ace part in the new H.G.T. Epic ...

A flash of music.

RADIO ANNOUNCER: This is station KNX, tomorrow night at nine-thirty in the Consolidated-Imperial-Tobacco programme Otto Stultz the famous H.G.T. film director will introduce you to ... Gail Howard!

Another flash of music.
CROSSFADE to second music.

FADE DOWN for studio noises.
There is a background of noises, voices, laughter, etc.
Suddenly, the voice of OTTO STULTZ, the director is heard.
STULTZ: Quiet! Quiet ... everybody!!! Silence...
MARKHAM: (*Irritated*) O.K. ... Otto, let's try it again!

LARRY: (*Shouting from the background*) Ready, Mr
                  Stultz!!!
JOE: (*Shouting from the background*) O.K., Mr
                  Stultz!!!
STULTZ: (*Quietly*) Music …
LARRY: (*Shouting*) Music!!!
JOE: (*Shouting*) Music!!!

The orchestra plays a gay waltz. The sound of a camera is heard.

STULTZ: (*Quietly*) Action …
LARRY: Action!!!
JOE: Action!!!

A pause.

The waltz continues.

TONY: (*A southern accent*) Why, Charlotte … why is it
                  you're not dancing, child? A pretty gal like you
                  should surely …
MARKHAM: (*Irritated*) Stop it!!! Stop it!!!
STULTZ: Stop! Stop!!!
LARRY: Stop!!!
JOE: Stop!!!

The music stops and so does the camera.

MARKHAM: What's the matter with Tony? He looks terrible!
TONY: Now what's the matter?
MARKHAM: Tony, you look awful! What the hell is it?
TONY: It's these confounded pants! Did they really
                  dress like this?
STULTZ: Sure!
TONY: Well, no wonder the North won!
MARKHAM: We've got to get this scene right, otherwise …
GAIL: Supposing I walk across towards the door as
                  soon as Tony …
STULTZ: No! No … you're swell. Just stay put …

169

MARKHAM: Give it a bit more … er … a bit more personality,
              Tony … Forget the pants … forget all about 'em
              … just act kinda natural.
TONY: O.K. …
STULTZ: Right … turn 'em over, Larry …
MARKHAM: (*Turning: irritated*) What is it, Doris?
DORIS: Mr Stultz wanted some water …
STULTZ: Water?
DORIS: (*Wearily*) For your dyspepsia tablet …
STULTZ: Oh, yeah! Now where the hell did I put those
              tablets?
MARKHAM: (*Impatiently*) Oh, have one of mine!
STULTZ: Oh, thanks. (*He drinks*) Go ahead, Larry!!!
LARRY: (*Shouting*) Music!!!
JOE: (*Shouting*) Music!!!
The waltz is heard again as is the camera.
A pause.
TONY: Why, Charlotte … why is it you're not dancing,
              child? A pretty gal like you should surely …
GAIL: I'm tired, Captain … Oh, so tired …
TONY: Tired? (*Chuckling*) What silly talk is this, my
              dear Charlotte? Tired? At your time of life …
              Give me your arm … Give me your arm, my
              child. Ah, that's better!
GAIL: What is the news tonight, Captain …?
TONY: News? Now, honey, don't go troubling your
              pretty little …
TONY is interrupted by a wild, hysterical scream from DORIS.
MARKHAM: (*Staggered*) For cryin' out loud!!! Stop!!!
LARRY: Stop!!!
JOE: Stop!!!
*The music stops. There is general consternation. The camera
noises stop too.*
GAIL: What is it …? What's the matter?

The waltz is heard again as is the camera.
A pause.

TONY:	Why, Charlotte ... why is it you're not dancing, child? A pretty gal like you should surely ...
GAIL:	I'm tired, Captain ... Oh, so tired ...
TONY:	Tired? (*Chuckling*) What silly talk is this, my dear Charlotte? Tired? At your time of life ... Give me your arm ... Give me your arm, my child. Ah, that's better!
GAIL:	What is the news tonight, Captain ...?
TONY:	News? Now, honey, don't go troubling your pretty little ...

TONY is interrupted by a wild, hysterical scream from DORIS.

MARKHAM:	(*Staggered*) For cryin' out loud!!! Stop!!!
LARRY:	Stop!!!
JOE:	Stop!!!

The music stops. There is general consternation. The camera noises stop too.

GAIL:	What is it ...? What's the matter?

170

TONY: Don't ask me!

MARKHAM: (*Angrily*) What is it, Doris? What the hell is the idea?

DORIS: (*Frightened and bewildered*) Look! Look ... Look at Stultz ...

There is a pause.

MARKHAM: (*Quietly*) What's the matter with him? Is – Is he asleep ...? Otto ... Otto wake up!

A tiny pause.

MARKHAM: Otto! Otto!!! (*Staggered*) My God! My God, he's dead!!!

There is a gasp of astonishment from the onlookers.

FADE In music.

Slow FADE DOWN music.

FADE IN the voice of CAMPBELL MANSFIELD.

MANSFIELD: Well ... Well, really ... I ... I mean to say!

DALLAS SHALE chuckles.

MANSFIELD: He was ... er ... dead, I suppose ...?

SHALE: Oh, yeah ... yeah ... quite dead.

MANSFIELD: But – But how did that happen ...? I mean, if ...

SHALE: Well, you see, Mr Mansfield, it was like this. When Margaret ... (*Suddenly*) Gosh! Is that clock right? Chee, if it is, I'd better be making a move ... Supposing we meet here next week Mr Mansfield, same ...

MANSFIELD: (*Interrupting SHALE*) That's all very well ... but what happens next week? You simply tell me another exciting ...

SHALE: Next week, Mr Mansfield, I'll – er – let you into a little secret ... I'll tell you who murdered Otto Stultz ... if it was murder.

MANSFIELD: You will!!!

SHALE: Yeah, an' Mary Brampton ... an' Leo Bartlett ...

171

MANSFIELD: (*Delighted*) You will!!! (*Suddenly remembering*) Yes, but ... what about Mr Hartington?

SHALE: Well, maybe I'll tell you who murdered Mr Hartington as well ... (*Chuckling*) You never know your luck! Goodnight, Mr Mansfield! Goodnight, Charlie!

The cuckoo clock announces the time.

Cuckoo! Cuckoo! Cuckoo! Cuckoo! Cuckoo! Cuckoo! Cuckoo! Cuckoo! Cuckoo!

END OF EPISODE SEVEN

EPISODE EIGHT

THAT'S MY STORY!

OPEN TO: Cuckoo! Cuckoo! Cuckoo! Cuckoo!
                   Cuckoo! Cuckoo! Cuckoo! Cuckoo!
A second clock chimes the hour.

DALLAS SHALE arrives.
SHALE: Hello, there! Say, am I late?
MANSFIELD: No – No, as a matter of fact, I'm rather early.
                   I've ordered you a drink.
SHALE: Oh, swell!
MANSFIELD: (*Raising his glass*) Well, er ... cheerio!
SHALE: Skoal! (*After drinking*) Now let's see – I got
                   to the part where they were shooting a scene
                   from The Sky Is Always Dark and Otto Stultz
                   passed out.
MANSFIELD: That's right. You – er – you said he was dead.
SHALE: Oh, he was dead, all right. There was no
                   doubt about that!
MANSFIELD: But – but was it murder?
SHALE: (*Laughing*) All in good time, Mr Mansfield
                   ... all in good time. Anyway, Doris
                   Charleston more or less took charge of the
                   proceedings and she sent for Divisional-
                   Inspector O'Hara. O'Hara arrived together
                   with a guy called Dr. Team. The doctor
                   examined the body and then O'Hara, Gail
                   Howard, Doris Charleston and the doctor
                   made their way towards a sort of general
                   dressing room which had been built on the
                   set. Gail was naturally rather bewildered by
                   this and she immediately asked the ... (*FADE
                   voice*)

FADE Scene.

FADE IN Scene.

GAIL: I suppose there's no doubt in your mind, doctor … about Mr Stultz being poisoned, I mean?

DR TEAM: (*Faintly amused*) None whatever, Miss Howard.

O'HARA: (*Puzzled*) Well, if he was poisoned then it must be suicide; I don't see how the devil it could be anything but suicide!

GAIL: (*Quickly*) Unless of course he was poisoned by the dyspepsia tablet …

DORIS: (*Surprised*) By the dyspepsia tablet …?

DR TEAM: Well, these are all right … perfectly harmless … they wouldn't even cure dyspepsia …

DORIS: (*Thoughtfully*) Just a minute …

O'HARA: What is it?

DORIS: Those tablets … the ones that Mr Markham gave to Stultz …

O'HARA: Yes?

DORIS: They didn't belong to Mr Markham …

O'HARA: (*Impatiently*) What do you mean now, they didn't belong to him?

GAIL: Who did they belong to?

DORIS: Mr Hartington …

O'HARA: (*Quietly: astonished*) Mr Hartington …?

DORIS: Yes.

O'HARA: I don't get this! What the devil would …

DORIS: Well, you see, Inspector, Markham took over Carnegie Hall, er – in other words Hartington's office, and a few days ago he lost his dyspepsia tablets. Markham was funny over little things like that – he'd throw away a hundred thousand dollars without even turning …

O'HARA: (*Impatiently*) Yeah … Yeah …

DORIS: Anyway, I simply couldn't find his dyspepsia tablets anywhere – I looked all over the office and

176

	suddenly I came across a bottle which had previously belonged to Mr Hartington – it was on a shelf on top of one of the bookcases.
O'HARA:	How do you know it had belonged to Mr Hartington?
DORIS:	Because Oliver … Because Hartington always kept his things there.
O'HARA:	I see. Did you tell Markham that the tablets were not … not his own?
DORIS:	Of course not!
DR TEAM:	This still doesn't solve the problem, does it? I mean – these dyspepsia tablets are perfectly all right, whether they belonged to Mr Hartington in the first place, or … or Laurel and Hardy.
O'HARA:	I agree, doctor! The tablets have got nothing whatever to do with the case.
GAIL:	(*Quietly*) Then how was Stultz poisoned?
O'HARA:	I don't know – that's one of the many things we've got to find out! Er … Miss Charleston, tell me … is it true that Miss Freeman was rather annoyed with Mr Stultz because she didn't – er – she didn't get the part of Charlotte Early?
DORIS:	Well, she wasn't exactly enthralled by the switchover to Miss Howard – shall we put it that way?
O'HARA:	I rather thought I saw Miss Freeman on the set when I arrived here.
DORIS:	Yes – she's talking to Louis Cheyne at the moment. Do you want a word with her?
O'HARA:	It might be quite an idea.
DORIS:	O.K.! I'll tell her.
DR TEAM:	Well, I'll be making a move. I'll send my report through the usual channels, but if you want me personally, O'Hara … just give me a ring.

O'HARA:	Thank you, doctor.

A tiny pause.

GAIL:	Inspector, you don't think that Margaret Freeman murdered Otto Stultz just because …
O'HARA:	Just because you happen to be playing … Charlotte Early? No. No, I don't think so. And even if she did … how the devil did she do it?
GAIL:	Do you think Stultz was murdered by the same …
O'HARA:	Oh, my God – don't say it! I can just see tomorrow's newspapers! Was Otto Stultz murdered by the same person that murdered Mary Brampton, Leo Bartlett and the great Mr Hartington?
GAIL:	Well – was he, Inspector?
O'HARA:	(*Softly*) I don't know. I've got a hunch – a wild sort of theory that might possibly amount to something. It rather depends on your young man.
GAIL:	(*Surprised*) Peter! What's Peter got to do with it?
O'HARA:	(*Slightly amused*) He's doing a spot of research for me at …
GAIL:	Research? Now what on earth does …
O'HARA:	(*Quietly*) Here's Miss Freeman …

A tiny pause.

MARGARET:	(*Quietly*) Good morning, Inspector.
O'HARA:	Good morning, Miss Freeman.
MARGARET:	Doris tells me that you … wanted to see me?

MARGARET has obviously been rather upset.

O'HARA:	Yes – there are one or two questions which I should rather like to ask you, if it isn't too much trouble.
MARGARET:	Please … please do.

O'HARA: I take it that you saw quite a great deal of Mr Stultz, Miss Freeman ... about the studios, I mean?

MARGARET: Yes. Yes, I suppose I did.

O'HARA: Well, perhaps you could tell me whether you noticed a change in him – quite recently, I mean.

MARGARET: A change? No. No, I don't think so.

O'HARA: He wasn't depressed at all ... or moody?

MARGARET: No. As a matter of fact, he seemed quite bright, and rather pleased with life. He was naturally delighted at directing The Sky Is Always Dark.

O'HARA: Yeah. Then in your opinion Mr Stultz didn't commit suicide?

MARGARET: Commit suicide? (*Amazed*) Are you serious? Of course he didn't commit suicide!

O'HARA: You seem very certain, Miss Freeman!

MARGARET: Why, good gracious me, of course I'm certain!

O'HARA: Then if he didn't commit suicide, what exactly do you think did happen?

A slight pause.

MARGARET: (*Quietly*) He was murdered ... murdered by the same person that murdered Mr Hartington ...

O'HARA: M'm ...

GAIL: It's quite obvious why Hartington was murdered – someone tried to sell him the film rights to Peter's novel at an outrageous price, and Hartington simply laughed at him ... or her. But why exactly was Mr Stultz murdered ... that's a different story?

O'HARA: Yeah – don't forget there must always be a motive, Miss Freeman.

MARGARET: You won't have much difficulty in finding a motive, Inspector. Plenty of people hated the sight of Otto.

179

O'HARA: Did you hate the sight of him?

MARGARET: Now isn't that rather a silly question?

O'HARA: But you had a row with Mr Stultz didn't you, Miss Freeman? Quite recently, I mean.

MARGARET: A row? What are you referring to? (*After a pause: candidly*) Listen, Inspector – I think I know what's at the back of your mind. You think I was annoyed with Otto because ... because he didn't consider that I was suitable for the part of Charlotte Early. That's right, isn't it?

O'HARA: That's right, Miss Freeman.

MARGARET: Well, I think there's something else you ought to know as well, Inspector ...

O'HARA: What's that?

MARGARET: It's simply the fact that when I saw Miss Howard on the set this morning I realised that she would be perfectly ... perfectly beautiful in the part. I told Otto this and ... and we became quite good friends again.

O'HARA: I see. (*Dismissing MARGARET*) Right, Miss Freeman ... thank you.

MARGARET: Good morning, Inspector. (*After a tiny pause*) Goodbye, Miss Howard ... don't let this dreadful business upset you too much ... you've – you've got what it takes, my dear!

GAIL: Thank you ... Margaret.

A pause.

O'HARA: M'm – was that an act or the real thing?

GAIL: Oh, she was perfectly sincere, Inspector, I'm sure of that.

O'HARA: I wonder. (*A tiny pause*) Ah, this is a damn queer business an' no mistake! Everything seems to point to suicide and yet ...

A pause.

GAIL:	(*Quietly*) O'Hara …
O'HARA:	Yes?
GAIL:	(*Slowly; thoughtfully*) I've been thinking about this Stultz affair and the Hartington business and … well … I think I know how Mr Hartington was murdered … and Otto Stultz.
O'HARA:	What …? What's that you say?
GAIL:	Listen, Inspector, we've all been trying to work out some fancy sort of theory as to how Mr Hartington was murdered, but you know, it may have been done very … very simply!
O'HARA:	What do you mean?
GAIL:	Hartington suffered from dyspepsia, didn't he?
O'HARA:	Yes. Yes, of course.
GAIL:	And he took dyspepsia tablets – large quantities of dyspepsia tablets. Now supposing someone inserted in a bottle of dyspepsia tablets one tablet which wasn't exactly meant to cure dyspepsia. It might be a day, it might be a week, it might even be three weeks before Mr Hartington took that particular tablet – but sooner or later he was bound to take it! and it so happened that he took it after …
O'HARA:	After a meal at The Blue Stetson! My gosh – I think you've got something!!!
GAIL:	But listen – and this is the point, Inspector … supposing this particular person wanted to make absolutely certain that Mr Hartington would take the tablet … now what would he do? He'd place a tablet containing poison in every bottle of dyspepsia tablets that Hartington possessed.
O'HARA:	But he'd only have one bottle, surely …
GAIL:	Oh, no – not necessarily. In fact he had at least two.
O'HARA:	How do you know?

GAIL:	Because Doris Charleston gave Markham the second bottle when she couldn't find his own. That's how Stultz was killed … by accident …
O'HARA:	Holy smoke … Markham handed Stultz the … how right you are!!! How right you are, my girl!!! Now, if only my hunch turns out to be o.k., we'll be sitting pretty …
GAIL:	Inspector, what is this hunch of yours? … Because if … (*Suddenly*) Hello … here's Peter! My word, he looks excited …

PETER arrives. He is both breathless and excited …

O'HARA:	Any news? …
PETER:	Yes … yes, you were right about Doris Charleston … Sergeant Moore actually discovered the details … Ancora Village, September 8th, 1924 …
GAIL:	(*Puzzled*) Peter … what is this?
PETER:	We'll explain later, darling …
O'HARA:	You heard about Stultz?
PETER:	Yes, my word what a shock it gave me.
O'HARA:	There's no doubt … about the details, I mean?
PETER:	No – none whatever.
O'HARA:	(*Thoughtfully*) Ancora Village, September 8th, 1924 … (*Suddenly*) Swell!!!
GAIL:	Ancora Village? … Where is that?
PETER:	About eighty miles the other side of Los Angeles …
GAIL:	But what's it got to do with Doris Charleston?
O'HARA:	(*Briskly*) We'll explain that later … (*To PETER*) I'll see you in about ten minutes, Peter.
PETER:	O.K.

A tiny pause.

GAIL:	You two seem very friendly.
PETER:	He's not a bad sort of guy when you get to know him. Darling, this Stultz business must have upset you terribly!

GAIL: It was rather a nasty shock – we were bang in the middle of a scene when it happened!

PETER: Good heavens!

GAIL: Peter – what is this mystery about Doris Charleston?

PETER: Well, the fact of the matter is, she … er … she doesn't happen to be Doris Charleston; at least, that was … that was her maiden name.

GAIL: (*Surprised*) Her maiden name …? Then she married …?

PETER: Yes.

GAIL: But – but who to …?

PETER: (*With a little laugh*) Well, I'm afraid this is going to be rather a shock, Gail, she was married to … Mr Hartington.

GAIL: (*Staggered*) Mr Hartington …?

PETER: (*Quietly*) Yes, to Mr Oliver Hartington … at Ancora Village on September 8th, 1924 …

FADE IN music.

FADE DOWN music.
FADE IN the voice of CAMPBELL MANSFIELD.

MANSFIELD: Why – why how perfectly extraordinary! Damn it, Shale, I … I can hardly believe it!

SHALE: (*Slightly amused*) Well, it was true, Mr Mansfield, don't make any mistake about that – as a matter of fact she admitted it.

MANSFIELD: (*Surprised*) She did …?

SHALE: Absolutely!

MANSFIELD: God bless my soul! Who – er – who did she admit it to … O'Hara …?

SHALE: (*Quietly*) Yeah …

MANSFIELD: (*Suddenly*) I say … Doris Charleston didn't … kill Mr Hartington … did she?

SHALE: Maybe I'd better tell you exactly what
                happened, so far as Doris Charleston is
                concerned.

MANSFIELD: By Jove, yes! Yes, by all means!

SHALE: Well, about two days later Julius Markham was
                directing Gail in a scene from The Sky Is
                Always Dark. I happened to be on the set
                talking to Louis Cheyne when O'Hara arrived.
                He seemed rather pleased with himself, I
                thought, and certainly made no attempt to …

FADE voice.
FADE In music.

FADE DOWN music.
CROSSFADE to studio noises and background.

MARKHAM: Listen, Gail … you … you haven't quite got it
                right … In this scene Charlotte isn't
                temperamental, it's more a sort of … well, I
                guess you'd call it petulance …

SHALE: Frankly, Julius, I don't like the dialogue.

LOUIS: I agree, Shale – it's kinda phoney!

MARKHAM: Well, who am I to criticise …? You boys wrote
                it!

GAIL: If you want my opinion, it isn't so much the
                dialogue as … (*Surprised*) Why, hello,
                Inspector …

O'HARA: Good afternoon … Good afternoon, gentlemen!
                I'm looking for Miss Charleston.

LOUIS: She was here a few minutes ago …

MARKHAM: (*Impatiently*) Miss what did you say …?

O'HARA: Miss Charleston.

MARKHAM: Oh, Miss Charleston … she's in my office.
                That's on block 4 … maybe you'd better take
                the Inspector along, Louis.

184

LOUIS: Sure! O.K. ... this way, Inspector.

O'HARA: Thanks.

FADE noises slightly.

LOUIS: Any news about the Stultz affair?

O'HARA: (*Pleasantly*) Don't you read the newspapers?

LOUIS: Not if I can help it.

O'HARA: (*After a pause*) Was Otto Stultz a popular sort of guy?

LOUIS: I suppose so.

O'HARA: Did you like him?

LOUIS: Not much. But then, I'm kind of choosey. This way, Inspector.

A door opens.

FADE.

FADE IN the opening of a second door.

A typewriter is heard. It stops when LOUIS and O'HARA enter.

O'HARA: Good afternoon, Miss Charleston!

DORIS: Oh, hello, Inspector!

LOUIS: I'll leave you two together. (*Laughing*) And you'd better know all the answers, Doris!

DORIS: (*Amused*) Don't worry, I'll make out!

The door closes.

O'HARA: I hope you're not too busy?

DORIS: Too busy ... for what ... Inspector?

O'HARA: Oh, just a little chat ...

DORIS: Will you have a cigarette – or are you on duty?

O'HARA: I'm on duty, but ... if you don't mind, I'll have a cigarette ... er ... one of my own.

DORIS: Sure. Any news about ... about ...

O'HARA: About Stultz? Yeah – the case is kind of sorting itself out ... But I didn't come here to talk about Otto Stultz, Miss Charleston, I er ... er ...

DORIS: What did you come to talk about?

A tiny pause.

O'HARA: About … Mr Hartington …

DORIS: (*Quietly; surprised*) Mr Hartington?

O'HARA: Yes. (*Suddenly*) Cigarette?

DORIS: No, no, thank you. (*A pause*) What – what about Mr Hartington?

O'HARA: (*Casually*) Have you got a light I … Oh, thanks! (*He lights his cigarette*)

DORIS: What – what about Mr Hartington?

O'HARA: M'm. Oh … about Hartington. He … er … He was married, did you know that? Yes, sir – Mr Oliver Hartington was married … September 8th, 1924 … Ancora Village. A kind of quiet wedding, I should imagine … wouldn't you?

A pause.

DORIS: (*Softly*) How did you find out?

O'HARA: Just a hunch … those counterfoils sort of first gave me the idea, an' then when you went off the deep end in that broadcast I sort of put two an' two together …

DORIS: (*Quietly*) I was seventeen when I married Hartington. We drove over to Ancora Village one night from Los Angeles – he was working as a barker in a funfair palace and … and … (*Suddenly*) God, how I learnt to hate and despise that man!

O'HARA: Why did you hate and despise Hartington?

DORIS: Because he was greedy, because he was selfish, and because he was as cruel as hell! We parted in 1927 and I went over to Europe for a short while – when I came back to America, which was in '32, I discovered that Hartington was in the picture business and going great guns. I asked him for a job and he agreed to give me one, on the condition that I remained silent so far as our marriage was

186

	concerned. I agreed to do so, but in 1939 I got into hot water ... financially, I mean ... and, well ...
O'HARA:	That explains the counterfoils?
DORIS:	Yes. But why shouldn't he have paid!! After all ... I was married to him, wasn't I?

A pause.

O'HARA:	(*Quietly*) Miss Charleston ... did you murder Mr Hartington?
DORIS:	No!! No!!! No!!!!
O'HARA:	But you murdered ... Leo Bartlett ... Margaret Freeman's ex-husband ...?

A second pause.

DORIS:	Yes. Yes ... I murdered Bartlett ... the swine was blackmailing me. He knew that I was married to Hartington and when Oliver was murdered he threatened to tell ... I got frightened. I thought if people knew that I was secretly married to Hartington then they'd naturally assume that I'd ... murdered him. But I didn't! I swear I didn't!!! (*Softly*) Although ... Although I intended to ...
O'HARA:	The cigarette you gave to Bartlett was originally intended for Hartington, wasn't it?
DORIS:	Yes ... Yes, I'd had it for weeks ... I almost slipped it into Hartington's case one night, but ... but at the last moment I became nervous and ... and changed my mind. Then when Leo Bartlett came to see me he placed his cigarette case on the desk, and ... well ... you know what happened.
O'HARA:	How did Leo Bartlett find out about your marriage to Hartington?
DORIS:	I don't know – that was always a mystery to me. There was only one person who knew, besides Hartington and myself, and ...
O'HARA:	And that was Mary Brampton?

187

DORIS: Yes. Yes … how did you know?

O'HARA: I didn't – at least not for certain, but I'd a pretty good reason for thinking so.

DORIS: What do you mean?

O'HARA: Bartlett was staying in Hollywood at The Garden of Allah – he'd been staying there off and on for several weeks, quite unknown to Margaret Freeman. Under an assumed name he was quite friendly with Mary Brampton and when Hartington was murdered she told him that …

DORIS: That I was married to Hartington and that she believed that …

O'HARA: That you'd murdered him … yes.

DORIS: (*Suddenly*) I see everything now! He murdered Mary and then started to blackmail me! I see everything, why …

O'HARA: (*Quietly*) Not quite everything, Miss Charleston. It's true that Bartlett murdered Mary Brampton … but … who … murdered … Mr Hartington!!!

DORIS: (*Desperately*) I don't know!! I tell you I don't know!!

O'HARA: (*After a tiny pause*) O.K., I guess we'll go down to headquarters.

DORIS: I'm … not … coming … down to headquarters, Inspector!

O'HARA: What do you mean? (*Suddenly*) Now don't be a fool … put that gun down! Put it down!!!

DORIS: Stand where you are!!! (*After a slight pause*) If you make one move, Inspector, I warn you, I'll …

O'HARA: Don't be a young idiot, you know darn well that you wouldn't shoot!

DORIS: Wouldn't I? Watch that mirror, Inspector, the one above your head!

A shot is heard and the mirror crashes to the floor.

O'HARA: (*Staggered*) Why ... Why you crazy young fool, I'll ... I'll ...

The door suddenly opens.

O'HARA: Look out!!! Look out, Peter!!!

PETER makes a wild dash across the room ... A shot is heard.

PETER: It's – it's o.k. ... I've got her!

GAIL: Careful, darling!!!

O'HARA: Be careful!!!

Another shot is heard and GAIL gives a sudden, startled cry ...

PETER: She's ... she's ... shot herself!!!

GAIL: Oh, Peter ... Peter ...

O'HARA: Get that cushion ... that's it ... quickly!

PETER: She's – she's trying to say something, O'Hara, listen ...

GAIL: Let me take her arm, Peter ... that's better!

O'HARA: Sh! Sh, quickly!!!

A tiny pause.

DORIS: (*Weakly*) O'Hara ...

O'HARA: Yes, Miss Charleston ...?

DORIS: I – I told you the truth ... I ... I never murdered Hartington ...

O'HARA: Then who did ...?

DORIS: I don't know ... I ... don't ... know ...

GAIL: (*Softly*) Oh, Peter ... Peter ...

FADE IN music.

FADE DOWN music.

We are once again, and for the last time, with CAMPBELL MANSFIELD and DALLAS SHALE.

MANSFIELD: (*Astonished*) And ... And she died ... Doris Charleston, I mean?

SHALE: Yes ... Yeah, I'm afraid so. She wasn't a bad kid either, judged from her own standards.

189

MANSFIELD:	So Doris Charleston murdered Leo Bartlett and Leo Bartlett murdered ... Mary Brampton. But – but who exactly murdered Mr Hartington?
SHALE:	(*Chuckling*) Well, now that's quite a question. But the way I figure it is this. When Mr Hartington first started to talk about buying the film rights of The Modern Pilgrim, someone in Hollywood – a guy who used to call himself Norman Roger Page – had a pretty good laugh, because he knew darn well that he possessed the film rights of The Modern Pilgrim and not Peter London.
MANSFIELD:	Yes ... Yes ... I understand that, but ...
SHALE:	Well, this guy Norman Roger Page ... who incidentally hated Hartington like hell ... confronted the old boy and told him quite bluntly that he wanted a pretty substantial figure for the film rights. Well, now ... Hartington didn't really want the film rights of The Modern Pilgrim, he simply wanted ...
MANSFIELD:	(*Faintly impatiently*) Peter London himself to take charge of the Scenario Department ... yes ... yes ... yes, I know all about that, but ...
SHALE:	But Hartington, who was a pretty cunning sort of reptile, knew that he'd got Norman Roger Page exactly where he wanted him, so he bought the film rights of The Modern Pilgrim for exactly ... sixty-seven dollars.
MANSFIELD:	Yes – yes, this is all very well, Shale – but ... but what I want to know is ... who is Norman Roger Page?
SHALE:	(*Amused*) The man who murdered Mr Hartington.

MANSFIELD: (*Exasperated*) Yes, but … who murdered Mr
               Hartington?

A tiny pause.
SHALE: I did.
A second pause.
MANSFIELD: You – you did …?
SHALE: (*Pleasantly*) That's right.
MANSFIELD: Then – then you're … Norman Roger Page …?
SHALE: That's right.
MANSFIELD: Oh … oh, I don't believe it. Why … why that's
               ridiculous … you're – you're joking!
SHALE: O.K. You don't have to believe it.
MANSFIELD: But – but … it's the most fantastic story I've
               ever heard, why … I mean …damn it all … I
               … I …
SHALE: (*Chuckling to himself*) Well, don't forget what
               you said eight weeks ago, Mr Mansfield …
               Hollywood has got to have new stories …
               Catch on? (*Brightly*) Goodbye, Charlie!
               Goodbye, Mr Mansfield!
MANSFIELD: (*Staggered, bewildered and confused*) Well …
               well, I mean to say …

FADE IN music.

FADE DOWN music.
1st AMERICAN: (*Pleasantly: surprised tone*) Hello, there! This
               is Jacki Wendleman, the voice of Hollywood!
               Welcome to Los Angeles, folks!!!
FADE UP music.

FADE DOWN music.
2nd VOICE: Variety!!! Flash! Gail Howard and Peter
               London take k.o. from Cupid … Life Sentence
               for H.G.T. star!

FADE UP music.

FADE DOWN music.

3rd VOICE: (*Friendly: jovial*) Don't forget to eat at Joe's Place. Mary had a little lamb, what will you have?

FADE UP music.

FADE DOWN music.

1st VOICE: Semi-tropical flowers, rich in fragrance and colour ...

2nd VOICE: White stucco houses and hospitable unfenced lawns ...

3rd VOICE: Arid desert and snow-capped mountains ...

FADE UP music.

FADE DOWN music.

1st VOICE: Cruel cactus, and friendly orange groves ...

2nd VOICE: The Trocadero ... Sunset Boulevard.

3rd VOICE: La Brea Avenue ... The Clover Club ... Harpo's Bar ... The Hollywood Punch Bowl.

4th VOICE: Wilshire Boulevard ... The Blue Stetson ... Charlie's Snuggery ...

3rd VOICE: Joe's Place ...

2nd VOICE: The Garden of Allah ... Ed's Taj Mahal Beanery.

FADE UP music.

FADE DOWN music.

MANSFIELD: (*Philosophically*) So this ... is Hollywood!

FADE UP music to a crescendo.

CROSSFADE to the cuckoo clock.

                Cuckoo! Cuckoo! Cuckoo! Cuckoo! Cuckoo! Cuckoo! Cuckoo! Cuckoo! Cuckoo!

THE END

Printed in Great Britain
by Amazon

10938346R00123